HELLIE JONDOE

HELLIE

TEXAS TECH UNIVERSITY PRESS

JONDOE

RANDALL PLATT

This book is typeset in Monotype Albertina. The paper used in this book meets the minimum requirements of ANSI/NISO Z39.48-1992 (R1997). ♾

Designed by Lindsay Starr

LIBRARY OF CONGRESS CATALOGING-IN-PUBLICATION DATA
Platt, Randall Beth, 1948–
    Hellie Jondoe / Randall Platt.
        p. cm.
    Summary: In 1918, as the Great War ends and the Spanish influenza pandemic begins, thirteen-year-old Hellie Jondoe survives on the streets of New York as a beggar and pickpocket until she boards the orphan train to Oregon, where she learns about loyalty, honesty, and the meaning of family.
    ISBN 978-0-89672-663-5 (pbk. : alk. paper)
    I. Title.
    PZ7.P7129He 2009
    [Fic]—dc22   2009021514

Printed in the United States of America
09 10 11 12 13 14 15 16 17 / 9 8 7 6 5 4 3 2 1

TEXAS TECH UNIVERSITY PRESS
Box 41037, Lubbock, Texas 79409-1037 USA
800.832.4042 | ttup@ttu.edu | www.ttup.ttu.edu

To my own partners in crime, S-J.S. and R-Dub

1

"Hellie, I think you killed him. Look at all that blood!" her brother said, kneeling over the body. "Great! Alls I need. Well, I ain't taking the fall for you, Hellie."

Hellie felt her knees weaken as though it was her own blood gushing forth. "How can he be dead?" she whispered, dropping her slingshot. She knelt down next to the man and touched his shoulder. "Mister? Mister, you all right? Harry, look there! He ain't dead!"

She reached into her pants pocket and pulled out a white satin scarf, swiped from an off-guard dowager just minutes before. She dotted her victim's bleeding forehead, then carefully bandaged the wound. "You're okay, mister." The man's eyes flickered.

"Hellie, come on! You ain't no nurse! He's coming 'round. Don't let him spot you."

"I got scared when he pulled a pistol on you, Harry." She picked up her slingshot and added, "Guess I'm stronger now I'm growing some."

Harry seized the slingshot. "Gimme that! I told you you're too young to tote."

"You tote a *gun* and you're only sixteen!" she growled back.

"Well, sixteen's three more than thirteen and you're a girl to boot! Come on!" Harry said, grabbing Hellie. She pulled away, snatched the man's hand, and started twisting a gold ring off his little finger. "*Now* what are you doing?" Harry said, looking over his shoulder.

"We ain't et proper in two days," she said, grunting as she pulled harder at the ring. The man, coming around, started to jerk his hand away.

"Cripes, Hellie! One minute you're healing him, next minute you're fleecing him!" Harry hollered from down the alley.

"Come on, mister! Give!" she said through gritting teeth. Then, seeing the glint of his gold watch fob peeping out from his vest pocket, she dropped his finger and, with the swipe of a seasoned pickpocket, snatched it all—fob, chain, and watch.

"Hellie!" Her name seemed to echo down the alley in harmony with the shrieks of the approaching police whistles.

The man opened his eyes to see the street urchin's dark and dirty face looking down at him. The jaunty cap, cocked atop the short, thick, matted hair, and the dirty face made the kid look more like his own corner newsboy, not the crying little waif who had lured him into the alley, set him up for a robbery, shot him in the head, and was now dangling his father's watch over his face.

"Thanks, mister."

His trembling hand went to his satin-wrapped forehead. "What happened?"

"You got a lesson and I got a watch." Her eyes landed on the pearl-handled pistol lying in the alley. "Oooo . . . and a gun. Double thanks!"

And she was off, pocketing his pistol and his watch, running after her brother and disappearing into the darkness of the New York alley.

Their gang numbered six—two teams of three—a wire, a lure, and a lookout. Pickpockets of the first degree. Not a one over the age of sixteen. They met at their current hangout exactly two hours after the alley mugging. The rules were clear—if something turns ugly, such as a mark pulling a gun and someone calling the cops, no one goes back to the hangout for two hours. Just in case.

"Dat damn little brudder of yours is gonna get one of us killed!" Archie, the oldest and self-proclaimed field marshal, said to Harry. "Him and dat slingshot of his!"

"Yeah, yeah, you don't need to tell me about it," Harry said. There was a noise outside their hideout. "Shhh!" The five gang members stared at the door. One drew a knife. Harry drew his pistol.

"Got food, beer!" Hellie announced as she pushed the door open and unloaded a box full of food on the barrel top that served as a table. Her eyes landed on her brother, and she said, grinning, "Got his clock and sling."

The boys pounced on the food like dogs, and, also like dogs, the larger, older boys got the lions' shares. Knowing this unwritten law, Hellie had leisurely eaten her own lion's share on the streets after pawning the gold watch.

"What'd it cop for?" Willie, a beefy Italian, asked, his mouth so full of cheese and bread that he could barely find room for the words.

"Three bucks," Hellie replied.

"Dis ain't three bucks' worth of food," C. K. said, drinking from the bucket of beer.

Hellie knew this law, too. Always, always bring some cash back for the gang. Otherwise it looked like you were holding out . . . being greedy, being stupid.

She dug into her pocket and deposited fifty-two cents on the barrel. When she felt the doubting eyes on her, she reached into her back pocket and pulled out another eleven cents.

"That all?" her brother demanded.

"What do you want for a three-buck thimble?"

She looked around, recalling the time these very same boys had beaten a seven-year-old for hogging. She pulled out the gold watch chain and handed it over.

"That's better," Harry said. "And don't you never shoot a mark over a stupid watch! Even with this toy!" He pulled her slingshot out from his pants and viciously hurled it at her.

Hellie caught it and said, "Slim ain't no toy."

"Da liddle wart's even got a name for it," Archie growled.

As they ate, Hellie kept toward the back of their waterfront shack, knowing the safest place with this fleet was sitting out of sight and out of mind while the others ate their fill. She sat with knees up, hat down low, just the way Harry had taught her.

Finally, Harry got up, counted out twelve cents from the take, and said, "Me and Hellie are thinking 'bout moving on."

"Moving on where?" Archie asked, tossing orange peels into a corner for the wharf rats to cart away.

Hellie watched her brother's face, the sparse candlelight casting long shadows on it. They had only briefly talked about leaving the gang, going out on their own. "I don't know. Thinking about moving west."

"Chicago?" C. K. asked. "Gonna be tough starting over in Chicago. You're better off here, where you know da streets."

"Where da streets know you," Willie quipped.

Then Archie said, "Tell you what. Ditch dat brudder of yours and maybe you and me can move up. I got a cousin what works a brace game uptown—nothing but rich saps uptown. Your looks, my connections—we'd make us a good con team. Ditch *all* dem rabbits." He pointed to the younger gang members with the knife he used to slice his orange.

Hellie looked at her brother's hardened face, curious for his reaction to the idea of ditching her. He gave her a casual glance and said, "Well, I'm always on the wake to new opportunities."

Hellie stood up, took her twelve-cent slice off the table, and said, "Suit yourself. I don't need none of you punks. I brung food, beer, and money, and you losers just take and eat."

"Thanks, Hellie," Flip said, holding up an orange. Flip was fourteen, looked ten, and was the quick and agile gopher of the gang since he could ease in and out of small places. Of the whole tribe, he was the only one besides her brother whom she might trust.

"You all know where you can go," she said, cocking down her cap and keeping her voice low and hard. She left and, once outside, grabbed a crate and crashed it against the hideout door.

Inside, Archie said to Harry, who was rising to follow Hellie, "Let da goonlet go. We're all bedder off widout him. 'Specially, you, Harry. Hellie's old enough to take care of hisself."

Harry opened the door to see Hellie disappear into the gray mist enveloping the wharf. "Yeah, I know," he said back to Archie. "Sometimes Hellie's more trouble than he's worth."

"Dump him," C. K. said. "He's got a short fuse and something about him ain't right." He tapped his forehead.

Harry knew it was only a matter of time before Archie and the rest would turn first on Hellie, then on him—like any pack that devours its weak. Sooner or later they'd figure out Hellie was a girl. Either he'd slip up or Hellie would. The last three gangs they'd hooked up with had been the same. Something had to be done about Hellie and soon.

C. K. stuck his knife into the barrel where it wanked back and forth. "Cut da apron strings, boyo. You'll never amount to nothin' wid Hellie 'round your neck."

Harry looked at the sets of cool and hard eyes staring back at him. Even little Flip's jaw was set, abiding by majority rule.

Harry showed the change in his hand. "I got more'n this coming to me."

Archie knocked his hand, and the money pinged into the dark recesses of the hideout. "Now you ain't even got dat!"

Harry pointed to Archie and said, "This ain't over!"

He could hear the hissing and crude laughter of the gang as he took off down the alley after his sister.

The streets of the Bowery at night didn't scare Hellie one snip. These streets were her school, playground, church. She knew every alley, dock, bridge, and hidey-hole. She knew which mission squawkers handed out food without making them pray for it, which flophouse managers turned their backs while a horde of kids scampered upstairs to share a room meant for two men, and which greengrocers looked the other way when a hungry kid pocketed a piece of fruit. She knew to stay off the whores' corners, to cross the street when a cop was approaching, to scope out street action from the reflection in a shop window, and to hide her face from the social workers who scoured the streets for homeless, helpless children. Hellie wasn't homeless *or* helpless. These streets *were* her home.

For nearly her entire life Hellie had worked these streets. She had known little else. Any memory of a home was a secondhand remembrance, doled out in small portions, like a precious winter orange, given in sections by her brother, Harry.

A sickly mother, a sailor father, a drunken grandfather—all tiny slices of something that, when Hellie tried to reassemble them, added up to nothing more than a blurry, lopsided memory of faded faces. All had died within six months of Hellie's second birthday. Four years with an aunt up in Connecticut who had five brats of her own to feed, and that was the end of their so-called family life. When she was six and

Harry was nine, they escaped the orphanage their aunt had finally deposited them in. Two days later, they'd made their way back to the city, learning at the feet of experienced Fagins, molls, and grifters and ganging in with street cruisers.

Since that time they had been on their own—just two more street arabs among the thousands, taking on life before life took them on. Each day was a lesson in survival and in human nature. For, as Harry had learned from a seasoned thief, one must know human nature in order to take advantage of the weaknesses in human nature. And by that early June of 1918, Harry had taught Hellie everything he knew.

Hellie crossed the street, hopped on the back end of a passing delivery wagon, and rode the fourteen blocks to their current lair, the cellar of a hemp factory, burnt out and boarded up a few months back.

Although the day had been warm, the cellar was chilly, dark, and damp and smelled of charred wood and old, moldy, water-soaked ropes that had crashed down from the upper stories during the fire. She heard a rustling and a squeak and knew it was just one of the dozens of rats and cats who shared the basement, startled by the strike of a match and the glow of a candle.

She took her cap off and tried to get her fingers through her filthy hair. She'd tried to get some soap and water through it after Harry last cut it and had to wonder how girls—real girls—ever managed with their long, lovely locks. She went to the cracked mirror hanging in the corner and rubbed it with her sleeve.

"You *are* stupid, Hellie!" she whispered, blue eyes staring into blue eyes. "How would you have felt killing that man over a cheap watch? You're about as bad as they come, Hellie Jondoe."

"That ain't no lie," Harry said, startling her.

"Get lost!" she returned. "Thought you and Archie was ganging in and heading uptown. Your looks? His connections?"

"You said it yourself. You're too stupid to be on your own."

Hellie turned and faced her brother. "You can leave any time you want. I can make it on my own, Harry. I don't need you."

"The hell you don't. If it wasn't for me, you'd be in the kids' pen. Or dead."

"How do you figure?" she challenged.

"Number one, you marked the wrong man tonight. Number two, you panicked when he pulled a gun. And with that, you stupid little funker!" He pointed to the slingshot swinging out of her back pocket.

She started to speak, but he cut her off. "Number three, you fell apart when you seen what you done." He imitated a high, whiny voice. "Don't die, mister! Please don't die!"

"I never said that!"

"Yeah? Where's that satin scarf you lifted off that old lady? What if one of the gang'd seen you go all girly over that man?" Again, he silenced her. "Number *four*, Hellie, you kept pawing him to get his watch! Let him get a good look at you and you knew the cops was coming!"

"We needed a score, Harry! And I noticed you eating your fill back at the shack."

Harry grabbed his sister by the shoulders and pushed her down onto a bed of charred rope. "You're dumb as a dead dog, Hellie! Didn't I learn you better? Didn't I?" He was coming at her with his fist. "You could of got us both killed!"

She leaped back up and faced him square. "But I didn't, did I? And look, I got his piece."

Harry grabbed the gun and held it up to her face. "If you'd had this and not your slingshot tonight, that man'd be dead and the cops would have dropped you on the spot! Probably me, too!"

"I'll hide it, Harry. I promise. We can hock it next time we're broke."

"You hide it good, then, Hellie!"

They locked eyes, as they had so many times lately. She was nearly a head and a half shorter than he was, but she had a way of leaning into a person that made her feel almost as tall as Harry.

"Hellie, long as you're with me, you'll do as I say! I king this family!"

"Go ahead and throw in with Archie! You and him'd last a whole day together. You two both think you're cock of the walk. Think I'll try things uptown myself. I hear a guy can do pretty good for himself clawing Broadway barons after midnight."

"Hellie, you ain't no 'guy.' You're a girl."

"Would you just make your mind up, Harry?" she cried. "One minute you tell me I have to act like a boy and then you up and remind me I'm just a dumb girl!"

"We've been through this."

"Why you always making me dress like this? Look like this? Then you get mad when I *act* like this!" She motioned to her clothes, her hair, her whole demeanor of a hard and solitary gutterpup.

He went to a carpetbag valise in which he hauled their few belongings when they moved from hovel to hovel. He reached in and pulled out two torn and faded photographs wrapped in paper and tied with a black ribbon. One was of a young girl, full of promise and beauty. The other was a young woman, that same girl, her promise of beauty fully realized, a startling look of coolness in her eyes.

He showed them to Hellie, who gave them a cursory glance and said, "Yeah, our mother. She's dead. So what?"

He moved the candle close to the mirror and told Hellie to look at the photos, then at her own reflection. "What do you see?"

"Best damn cannon of moveable property between Satan's Circus and Hell's Kitchen."

"I'm serious, Hellie."

She took a look and replied, "I see Hellie Jondoe."

"Helena Smith," he corrected, looking into her eyes in the mirror's reflection.

She formed a fist and shouted, "Don't you never call me that! That name ain't me! I'm Hellie Jondoe. You baptized me that yourself after my first run-in with the cops. Remember? And I kept my trap shut and didn't cry or nothing. You said we're both Jondoes to the world."

"Don't matter what you call yourself, Hellie. Can't you see how much you look like her? You're changing."

Hellie moved the photos next to the candle and compared herself to her mother's raven hair, olive complexion, and intense eyes that seemed to burn through the photograph. She rubbed some soot off her cheek. "I don't want no change, Harry. I want things to be just like this. For always."

"Now you understand why I make you pretend you're a boy? The hoods we run with, the way we live . . . Hellie, if they knew what's about to spring from under all that . . ." He indicated her clothes, then her face. "Hellie, you're comin' in pretty. I see little changes every day."

Hellie sat down, trying to understand. "Yeah, but . . ."

"Hellie, there's only one thing a girl becomes around here. And the sooner she shows pretty, the sooner she becomes one."

Hellie looked at the photo of their beautiful mother. "Like she was?"

Harry took the photo and looked at it. If looking could wear an image away, then this photograph would be a gray, faceless shadow. "Don't matter what she was. She's dead. But you're alive. That's why I quit the gang tonight."

"Now Hellie, you just shut up and listen. It's just a free ticket out west. Nothing else!"

"I ain't going! *You* go. *You* go be a orphan! I think you're the dumb one, Harry. From now on, you got no right ever to call me dumb again!"

Hellie kept walking, kicking a can as she did. A street dog sniffed the can, and she pulled out her slingshot, grabbed a rock, and took aim.

"Don't you shoot that dog, Hellie!" Harry said, grabbing for the slingshot.

"I ain't shooting the dog, I'm shooting . . ." she pulled the sling back, closed one eye, and let the rock fly. Whank! The tin can jumped and the dog yelped in surprise. ". . . the can." She looked at her brother and added, "You know I like dogs. I'd have me one if you'd let me."

"Two mouths is enough to fill," Harry said.

"Think it's hot enough for a swim? Want to head down to Coney?"

"No, we got other things to do. Come on," Harry said, pulling Hellie.

"Where?"

"And I don't want to hear no screaming," Harry said.

Hellie pulled to a stop and whipped Harry around. "Screaming about what?"

"We got to get some orphan train plans together."

Hellie backed up. "I mean it, Harry! I don't want nothing to do with that orphan train business. We tried being orphans. Remember? When we was short ears? Ran away! That's how much we liked being orphans!"

Hellie stopped in front of a poster pasted to a storefront window. "Say, ain't she pretty?" she said. "Look, Harry."

The poster was of a beautiful young mother, her babe in arms, gossamer gown wrapped around her lithe body, long hair drifting upward in a sea of green.

"What's it say, Harry?"

He read the one word. "En . . . list. Enlist. Ah, it's just advertising for the war, Hellie. Come on."

"No, I'm lifting it," she said, pulling at a corner. "It's a pretty picture."

"It's a dead drowned mother and baby, Hellie. You don't want that."

"Sure I do. You know I like pictures."

"Come on!"

Hellie ripped the poster down, folded it and stuffed it into her pants, then ran to catch up with Harry.

A fruit-cart vendor grew suspicious of them, standing so close to his apples, and shooed them along with a push against Hellie's shoulder. She pushed back, they scuffled some, and then she laughed and ran to catch up with her brother. She handed him an apple and took a bite out of her own. The vendor was screaming something in Italian and shaking his fist.

Harry devoured the apple, not so much out of hunger, but out of street habit—you eat when you have it. They settled on a park bench and watched the squirrels, rushing about with street habits of their own.

Harry pulled out the flyer again and unfolded it. He labored over the words he could read. Hellie looked over his shoulder. "That there says 'Wanted: homes for children,'" he explained, pointing to the largest print at the top of the flyer.

"Where'd you get this?" Hellie asked. "Salvation Army or some Jesus-shouter?"

"Never you mind where I got it. You just sit and listen to what it says. It says we can get put on a train west. Free."

"As orphans, Harry. You said it was on the orphan train. Hell, I'll crawl west on my stomach before I'll be a orphan again."

"It's just a con, Hellie."

"I don't want to go nowhere, free train ride or not! I ain't leaving New York!" Her large blue eyes were wide and serious.

"We both need us a new start, Hellie. We're gonna die young on these streets. Remember last winter? You took sick?"

"It was just a cold. Everyone gets colds. You got sick, too, you know."

"Hellie, you ain't seeing this right."

"No!" she hollered, ignoring the glances of two elderly men playing checkers in a patch of sunlight. "*You* ain't seeing this right! I know you, Harry! I know what you're up to!" Tears heated her eyes, but she forced them back, keeping to her childhood pledge to never, ever, let anyone see her cry, especially Harry. "You're going to get me out west and then you're going to evaporate! You ain't looking for a new start. You're always griping at me for sticking to you like a shadow! You just want me out of the way so's you and Archie can team up!"

"Hellie! That's a lie! I want us both to get out of here. West is where we need to be. Not here! Not no more!"

She continued walking, but Harry pursued. "Hellie! You listen to me! I'm doing this for both us. Look, I been to these folks." He whirled her around and put the flier in front of her face. "I set it all up. They're square shooters. So we're both getting on that orphan train. We're going west, and I figure once we're there, we're jumping off. Starting over. Just you and me. Some nice place like Wichita or maybe even farther west. Maybe Denver. Maybe Frisco! Timbuktu for all I know! Hellie, we go along with the orphan bit, find us some chumps to take us on, and then we walk. What's wrong with that? It's a perfect way out."

"No!"

They stared at each other for a moment. Hellie thought she knew Harry, his every glance, his every grin, his every stance. But this was all new to her. This sudden enthusiasm. This sudden passion for any place west of Mott Street.

"I *dare* you, Hellie."

She bit her lip and narrowed her eyes. Had she ever backed down from one of Harry's dares? She slowly nodded her head and said, "Okay,

I take your dare and I dare *you* one! I dare you to come back with me the minute I tell you I hate it out west."

"You ain't going to hate it, Hellie. You wait and see."

"You shake on the dare or I ain't budging from this very spot, Harry." She spit in her hand and offered it to her brother.

He spit in his and they shook on it.

"Jesus, Joseph, and Mary! Where did you get all that mazuma?" Hellie exclaimed, looking at the handful of cash Harry pulled out from behind a loose brick in the hemp cellar wall a few days later. She fingered the coins in their neat small stacks and sifted through the dollar bills. "How much is that?"

"One hundred and fifty-two dollars and seventy-three cents. And look. A brand-new fifty-dollar bill."

"I never seen so much money all in one place." Then she stepped back and said, "Harry, what did you . . . ?"

"I weeded it from that kitty Archie hides in the oil barrel, the one in the corner. He thinks he's so smart. I spotted that stash of his the first week we ganged up."

"But Harry, you know Archie. He'll come looking."

"I just raked our share. I knew Archie'd been cutting the melon in his favor," Harry said, putting the cash back into the hiding spot.

"He'd kill you just as soon as look at you to get it back."

"He don't scare me. Besides, he don't know about this place. And by Saturday, we'll be long gone, remember?"

Then Harry went to the cellar steps where he had hidden a large canvas duffel underneath. He plopped it at Hellie's feet and said, "Here."

"What's all that?" Hellie asked with a suspicious glance.

"Girl clothes. Got 'em at some secondhand store."

"Hope they fit *you*, 'cause I ain't wearing no girl clothes!"

"The hell you ain't! Who'd adopt a snipe looking the way you do?"

Hellie kicked the duffel and said, "Ain't wearing 'em!"

"And quit saying 'ain't'! It ain't . . . isn't . . . good English. Folks don't like girls talking ignorant."

"Ain't! Ain't! Ain't!"

"I knew this would happen," he said.

"Ain't nothing in that duffel that's going to change me, Harry!"

Harry formed a fist and said, "I'd knock your block off, Hellie, but black eyes don't look good on orphans."

Hellie raised her own fists. "Go ahead! You just try!"

Harry ignored her challenge. "And there's some lye soap and rose water in that duffel. Haul some water so's you can get some of that stink off you."

"You smell worse than me! What about you?"

"I got better things to do if we're getting us on that train tomorrow. Now, you go on and sort out all this stuff." He shoved the duffel toward Hellie. "I'll be back by nightfall."

Hellie watched her brother run up the cellar steps. Resigned, she sat down and carefully opened the duffel and began pulling things out. She winced when she smelled the bar of lye soap, but smiled when she took in the breezy, carefree aroma of the rose water. An ever-so-fleeting glimpse of a warm, kind woman in her past wafted through the hemp cellar.

She hauled two buckets of water from the barrel outside and washed up in a dark corner of the cellar. Getting her comb through her matted hair was the toughest part, but a rose-water rinse helped.

Hellie carefully smoothed the blanket on her sleeping pallet, slapped off as much dust and dirt as she could, and carefully laid out the clothes. Three dresses and two skirts, hose, a pair of button boots, gloves, a coat, and a hat.

Then, with a cautious glance around to make sure Harry wasn't near and the rats weren't looking, she put the showy green taffeta dress up to her and looked into the mirror. She looked at the buttons that marched up the back and wondered how one got into or out of these things.

She tossed the green mass onto her bed and pulled on one of the skirts—blue and white with a lace hem—not sure if the buttons went in front or back. She whirled a bit to watch the dress fan out as she spun. Then she picked up the boater hat. Wide-brimmed, light yellow straw, large blue ribbon falling down the back. She put it on and looked at her reflection and stuck her tongue out at her image. She floated around and let the long ribbons chase her in a fun, fast circle. "Moiy I have this dance, Loidy Astorbilt?" she said in mocking English accent. "But of course, Lord . . ."

She didn't hear the cellar door open. She looked up and stopped cold when she saw Harry. Archie was behind him, holding a gun to his back.

"Hellie," Harry said, his voice very low and controlled, "you do just like I say, you hear?"

"Shut up!" Archie said, giving Harry a shove down the steps. He looked at Hellie and asked, "Now what do we have here?"

The rest of the gang eased in, each letting his eyes adjust to the darkness, the smoky residue odor, and the scene unfolding below. Hellie's blood stopped cold.

Hellie quickly took off the hat and let it slip from her hand. Archie poked Harry toward her. Hellie kept her eyes on Harry's face while Archie looked her up and down. "What sort of . . . wait a minute!" Then he started to laugh and said, "Damn! Looky here, boys, we got us a coupla Lizzie boys."

As many times as Hellie had had to read her brother's face in a tricky situation, she was now at a loss. She moved to say something, but Harry cut her off. "Hellie, don't you say a word. Let me do the talking. Okay, Archie, I'll get your money and you and your crew just move on."

"But dat was before I knew what kind of 'men' I was working wid."

Hellie began to laugh. "He thinks we're . . . what? *Queer?* That's the funniest thing I ever heard!" She put her head back and roared. Her knees buckled and she rolled on her bed, crushing the clothes.

"What's he laughing at?" Archie asked.

Harry cried, "Hellie! This ain't funny! This ain't no popgun on my back!"

She kept rolling and laughing until her hand touched the cool metal tip of the pistol she had taken off her mark in the alley a week ago. She finally sat up, sure that the layers of dresses were high around her and her hidden weapon. She caught her breath finally and looked up at Harry and Archie.

"Joke's on you, Archie," she said, pointing her finger. "I'm his sister, not his brother . . ." She started to laugh again. C. K., Willie, and Flip were hesitantly chuckling.

Archie was not laughing, and his response was to shove Harry toward Hellie and hold the gun now on both of them. When Harry fell next to Hellie, she caught his eye and, passing him the gun under the green taffeta billows, added, "Harry, don't you see how funny that is?"

Harry felt the gun and said, "Well, I guess it is funny. It's true, Archie. Hellie's a girl. She's a plug-ugly little runt so it don't much matter."

"Prove it," Archie said.

All laughing ceased.

"What?" Hellie asked, her smile now vanished.

"What do you think, boys? Ever been to a strip burlicue?"

"Hellie, you don't move a muscle," Harry ordered. "Knock it off, Archie. Joke's over. I'll get your money and you boys leave."

"Stand up," Archie said, the gun now aimed at Hellie.

Hellie started to get up, and Harry pulled her back down.

"Archie, stop it . . ." Flip said, coming down the steps toward them.

"Shut up. Come on, *sister*. Make me a believer."

Hellie shook loose of Harry's grip and stood up. "I think Archie liked me better when I was a boy."

Archie raised his hand to hit Hellie and Harry stood up, Hellie's pistol aimed squarely at Archie. "You step away, Hellie," he said.

Archie grabbed Hellie's skirt, jerked her toward him, and held her tight, the gun to her head. "Put it down, boyo. I'll kill her. In a heartbeat."

"Archie!" Flip cried.

Harry let the pistol fall from his hand. "Let her go," he said.

"You just get my money," Archie said, tightening his grip around Hellie's chest. "Hmm," he whispered into her ear, smelling the rosy scent of her hair. "Guess maybe you are a girl."

Hellie elbowed him in the gut, and Harry swooped the pistol off the floor. Hellie fought Archie for his gun with all her might. The guns discharged simultaneously. Harry went down. Archie fell forward.

"Let's get outta here!" C. K. hollered as he and Willie scrambled out of the cellar. Flip rushed to Hellie and Harry.

"Harry!" Hellie screamed, going to him. He fell into the green taffeta dress, which fluffed up around him.

Archie was at her feet. Dead.

Hellie had never been inside a hospital. All their childhood ills and injuries were handled at the free clinic next to the Bowery Salvation Army. Saint Anne's Charity Hospital was white, cold, and smelled of infection, antiseptic, and death. Nuns in stiff white smocks and odd-cornered hats scurried down the halls, consulting with doctors and avoiding Hellie's frightened, eager glance.

She found a bathroom and cleaned the dried blood from her hands and face. She finally scavenged a half-eaten sandwich from a trash can and dozed on a bench in the ladies' room, newspapers as her blankets.

When she awoke, Hellie followed a nurse whose rubber shoes echoed an efficient squeak down the hall. "Ma'am? Ma'am? How's Harry? How's my brother?"

"Don't you think you should go home?" the nurse said. "It's five in the morning."

"My brother. Harry. They brought him in last night. Can I see him?"

The nun looked into Hellie's exhausted, anguished face and took pity.

"Gunshot wound?"

"Yes! That's him. Can I see him?"

The nurse sighed, then said with a resigned whisper, "All right. Come with me. But only for a minute."

Hellie followed the nurse down the hall, past a black man slopping a steaming antiseptic onto the floors, into a large ward with rows of beds separated into tiny cubicles by cloth partition panels.

The nurse moved the panel and shined her flashlight on Harry's sleeping face. "That him?"

"Yes. He gonna be okay?" Hellie whispered.

The nurse picked up the chart at the foot of his bed, put her flashlight on it, and stated, "Serious condition. Bullet wound to upper left chest. Surgery scheduled for 8:00 a.m. Bleeding stopped. Patient sedated." She replaced the chart and shook her head. "Lord Almighty, these street hoods get younger every day." Another patient groaned, and she went across the ward. Hellie carefully approached Harry. She pulled the light cord that offered a sickly incandescence.

Hellie looked at Harry. He seemed to have melted into the bed, tucked tightly in on all three sides. His head was neatly nestled into the stark white pillow, and his face was sallow and gray.

"Harry," Hellie whispered, as though she was a kid again, waking him up to escort her to the outhouse. "Hey, Harry . . . ?" He didn't move. She looked at him and noticed how his chest barely moved under the sheet, how his breath barely came. "You're gonna be fine." She sat on the chair next to Harry, placed her head on the bed, and cried uncontrollably. "I lied, I can't take care of myself, Harry. You gotta take care of me."

There was a slight movement from under the covers. Harry's head moved just slightly. Hellie quickly ran her sleeve over her face as Harry opened his eyes.

"Harry, I shouldn't have run out!" she gushed. "Flip ran for help, but when the sirens got near, I got, I mean, well, Archie was dead and . . ."

"That's okay," he whispered. "You did right. But Hellie . . ."

"I killed him. Guess I finally botched things good."

"No, Hellie. Stop talking and listen to me."

"Well, I ain't gonna run out on you again, Harry. I'm sitting right here till you're good enough to get out."

"No, Hellie. You got to get out of here. The cops . . ."

"I know. There were two in the hall after they got you here. I hid in the ladies' can."

"Listen to me, Hellie," Harry said, fighting to keep awake under the sedation. "That canvas sack under my bed. My coat. Get that paper in the pocket."

She extracted the paper and recognized it as the flier about the orphan train. "No, Harry! I ain't going! Not without you!" She wadded the paper up and threw it on the floor.

"Yes, you are! Now Hellie, you just listen. Cops was here asking questions. I didn't spill anything. But don't you see? C. K. and Willie saw it all and they *will* spill."

"I ain't scared and I ain't running," Hellie said.

"You be on that train and I'll come find you. I promise. Soon as I'm out of here. You leave me some of that money we got hid."

"No!"

"Hellie, anything happens to me, the cops'll make you go to some orphanage anyway. Maybe even a girls' reform nursery. Can't you get it through your thick head?" His face contorted in pain.

"You have to go now," the nurse said to Hellie, coming to Harry's bedside. "Look, you've started the bleeding again." She filled a syringe and gave him a shot. Then, to Hellie, said, "I've given him morphine so he'll sleep. You have to leave. Come back by noon tomorrow. After surgery."

"I don't want to go," Hellie said, sounding more like a child than she had in the past five years.

"He is very sick and needs his strength," the nurse added.

"I ain't going, Harry, and you can't make me."

"Yes I can," he whispered, his face starting to soften, his eyes closed. "You're going to do what I tell you, you little creep." His voice got blurry. "I'll come find you . . ."

"You won't find me, Harry," Hellie said, feeling that small ache deep down inside growing.

"Come along now," the nurse said, urging Hellie away.

"Sure, I'll find you," Harry whispered, a small smile coming to his lips. "Wait and . . ."

"No, you won't," Hellie whispered back as the nurse escorted her out of the ward.

Hellie crept downstairs, surveying each corridor and alcove for police or, worse yet, social workers. Little by little, the events of the night were creeping into her head, playing out in slow motion, like she'd seen in a movie once. And, also like a movie, it was as though the film broke, leaving the scene frozen in time . . . the fight with Archie, the scuffle, the gunshots, the green taffeta dress. Each scene frozen. What happened? Harry's blood. Archie's blood.

She was shaking her head, hoping the scenes would just fall out and let her think. Now what? Now where?

A ruckus at the main entrance made her stop and peer around the corner. Two cops were dragging a bloody and boisterous drunk. Hellie slipped through the first open door. The room was dimly lit and oddly silent.

"Please don't let this be the morgue," she whispered, waiting for her eyes to adjust to the dark. When her eyes beheld an altar adorned with rows of small candles flickering a dancing light up to a large golden crucifix, she realized she was in a chapel.

She heard footsteps approaching and ducked into the small closet not far from the altar. She watched one of the policemen through the thin slats in the closet door. His hat was under his arm, and he crossed himself with holy water as he entered. He knelt before the pew, crossed himself again, proceeded to the altar and lit a candle, then returned and sat in a pew and prayed on bended knee.

Hellie's heart rapped against her ribs, but nearly leaped out when a voice said, "Yes, my child?"

Hellie whipped around and whispered, "Who's there?"

"Father Thompson." There was a pause, then he said, "I'm sure I don't need to remind you of the hour. So please, go ahead."

Hellie looked through the slats and saw the cop was still praying. The little hatch opened and Hellie said, "Oh. You're a priest?"

"That usually is what you find on this side of the confessional." His voice was low and Hellie thought he was stifling a yawn. "How long has it been since your last confession?"

Hellie looked at him through the screen, noticing his elderly profile looking down as though he was cleaning his fingernails. "I ain't confessing nothing. I'm hiding," she said.

"Ah. Sanctuary?" he asked. Hellie could hear a tinge of mockery in his voice.

"No, I'm *hiding*," she whispered.

His voice hardened. "Look, kids come in here all the time on a dare or as a joke and I'm in no mood for either. Now, do you want to confess something or not?"

The policeman showed no sign of finishing his heavenly communication.

"Yes."

"I'm listening."

"I killed someone last night." She found it slipping out so fast, she put her hand to her lips. She could feel the priest's eyes on her now.

"You what?"

"Do you make it right?" she asked.

"How old are you?"

"Old enough to go to hell, I guess," she said.

"Uh huh. You *killed* someone?" the priest asked. Hellie could tell a doubting adult, even in a darkened room.

"Does it matter if it's self-defense or if he deserved it?"

"If this is some sort of prank, I warn you, God will . . ."

Hellie heard a noise from the chapel and peeked out to see the policeman finally finish his prayer. "Look, I gotta go. Just quick tell me if you can make it right. And can you make it so's my shot-up brother lives? I know that's a lot, but could you, Mister Father?"

"What's your name?"

"Oh, no you don't . . ." Hellie stood up.

"Are you even Catholic?" the priest said, exhaling wearily.

"No. But that don't mean I ain't scared to death of going to hell for what I done."

"If what you say is true, I will pray very hard for you and your brother," he said. "If it's not . . ."

"So I'm forgiven if I killed someone, but not if I'm lying about it?"

"Do you have anything else to confess, my child?" the priest asked. "This is a hospital and I have a lot of people to pray for."

Hellie got up to leave. "That's all. Say, this here's just between us, right?"

"Well, between you and me and *God*."

Hellie paused, her hand on the confessional door latch. "Guess I'll just have to trust you."

She left, carefully easing her way out of the hospital without being spotted.

Hellie, exhausted and confused, went back to the hemp cellar. She stopped cold when she saw the cellar door ajar. Had she remembered to close it last night in all the horror and confusion? She nudged it open farther and waited for her eyes to adjust to the slim light coming in through the high, street-level windows.

It was as though a dervish had whirled in through the holes in the ceiling and inspected every corner. The pallets were turned over, and their few belongings were scattered about and tromped upon. The green taffeta dress, now a mass of blood-dried billows, was hanging from a piece of rope from a beam, like a jilted bride had hanged herself there.

She knew it was the work of C. K. and Willie . . . looking for their loot, maybe retaliating for Archie. She walked around her scattered clothes and the dried pools of blood toward a beam where the two photographs of her mother were stabbed by a rusty knife. She pulled it out, tried to smooth the gash in the photos, and knew exactly the message C. K. was leaving.

Her heart pounded as she quickly gathered her things from around the room. She slipped out of her skirt, stained with Harry's blood. She stepped into the familiar comfort of her filthy pants, shirt, and jacket. Finally, she pulled the loose brick in the wall and extracted Harry's stash of money. She held the crisp fifty-dollar bill, thinking out loud, "He'll need that when he comes west to find me." She paused, reconsidering.

"Harry ain't coming to find me," she said down to the face on the bill. But she put it back, replaced the brick, hid her money in the bottom of the carpetbag valise, and continued packing.

She found some bread and cheese and remembered how hungry she was. She ate while sitting on her pallet, scratching absently at the blood-stains on the ticking. She leaned back, unable to keep her eyes open.

"Hellie! Hellie! Wake up!"

Hellie startled awake, stood up, and instinctively grabbed her sling-shot and took aim at Flip. "You with C. K. and Willie?" she demanded.

"Hellie, no!" Flip cried, putting up his hands to protect his face. "Don't shoot! I gotta tell you something."

She kept her aim and said, "Cause if you are, swear to God, I'll shoot!"

"It's Harry. I got to tell you. I just come from da hospital." Flip slowly brought his hands down. "Harry's dead. Died getting dat bullet tooken out."

"You're lying!" Hellie shouted, pulling back her slingshot. "You're a damn liar!"

"No, Hellie. I'm sorry. It's true. I just come from dere."

"I'm going to see for myself!" Hellie said, pushing past Flip.

Flip caught her elbow and pulled her around. "Hellie! Listen to me. Da boys, C. K. and Willie . . . dey're after you! Look at dis place. You think da cops did all dis?"

"I don't care about the gang or the cops. Harry's not dead! I was just there a few hours ago."

"And I was dere when they took him in to operate. Here, Harry said give you dis." He pulled out the crumpled flier and handed it to her. "It's about dat orphan train."

"He told you about it?"

"Yeah. Few weeks ago. I don't even got a tribe no more. C. K. and Willie'd just as soon kill me as look at me, now. You too, Hellie. We're both marked."

"Harry's dead?" Hellie whispered finally.

"I'm sorry, Hellie. I got his jacket and stuff outside. You want it?"

"No," Hellie whispered. Hellie couldn't read the flier, but she knew she was in a tight spot. Maybe this was her only salvation. Harry's last warnings to her echoed through her stunned mind. His promise to find her sifted away like sand sifts through one's tight grasp.

"You gotta move faster," Flip finally said. "C. K. and Willie . . . you know dey'll be back. And that orphan train leaves today!"

All there was left to pack were the photos of her mother. She went to the hiding spot and pulled out the fifty she had left for Harry. "That's that, then. Here, Flip, you're gonna need this," she said.

"Fifty dollars? All on one piece of paper!"

"You got to duck out, too. Use it to get somewheres. Don't you got that sister over in Jersey?"

"Nah, she got married and don't want me around. Thanks, Hellie," he added, taking the money. "I always liked you, Hellie. Boy, girl, or something in between. You always stuck up for me."

Hellie snapped the valise closed and took a look around the cellar.

"Here. Don't forget ol' Slim," Flip said, handing her the slingshot.

Flip escorted Hellie out of the alley and onto the street. There were no last looks back. Never have been, never will be, she thought. The ache in her stomach was as foreign as it was unsettling.

Flip stayed with her while she got a hansom cab. She showed the driver the flier with the address of the Society for Friendless Children. She turned to tell Flip so long, but he had vanished.

Flip stood behind a car and watched her leave before turning and walking through the shadows back to Saint Anne's Charity Hospital.

"You do like I tell you?"

"Worst lie I ever told in my whole, entire life. But I did it."

"She believe you?"

"Not at first. She called me a liar. Which I am," Flip said, an impish smile coming to his small, freckled face. "But I poured it on pretty thick and she finally got da picture."

Harry sat straighter up in his bed, wincing as he moved his bandaged shoulder and torso. He lit a hand-rolled cigarette and said through the exhaling smoke, "Good then. That's that."

"Oh, here," Flip said, pulling the fifty-dollar bill out of his pocket. "She said I'd be needing dis. Felt bad about taking it, but I reckon you and me is going to need it."

Harry looked at it. "Huh. Funny. Fifty bucks. It's the same fifty they gave me for Hellie."

"You *sold* Hellie?" Flip asked, his jaw dropping.

"Take it easy. They called it a 'finder's fee.' It's all legal. Hell, it's not like it's slavery or nothing. Adoption ain't slavery. Hellie needs a mother, so don't look at me like that. That fifty bucks buys her a mother and it buys me a new start."

Flip sat down next to Harry and lit his own cigarette. "Still, you should have seen her face when I told her you was dead. It was like she broke all into little pieces. I never felt lower in my whole life."

"Hellie don't have a Chinaman's chance here in the city. The cops, C. K., and Willie all looking for her. I tell you, that orphan train is the best for all of us. Anyway, every man for hisself on the Bowery. No place for girls anyhow."

"Hellie a girl," Flip said. "Huh. Sure had me fooled."

"Well, everyone was going to figure it out sooner or later. Girls change, you know. They become dames. That's why I had to send her away."

"Sure."

"Here, change this fifty and keep half, Flip. You earned it. Once I get out of here, should be in a week or so, you and me, we'll double-team, okay? You got a good hidey-hole?"

"Got a place, nice and quiet, right here. A storage closet across da hall from where dey put da stiffs."

"Good. Stay low. You been a pal, Flip. I won't forget this."

Flip sighed as he crushed out his cigarette on the bedside ashtray. "Worst thing I did in my whole life telling Hellie you was dead."

"She'll get over it," Harry said. "Hellie's tougher'n rawhide and she'll be fine out west. And she ain't likely to come back, neither."

"Won't be the same widout Hellie."

"Nope. It'll be better. For all of us."

The cab pulled up to a three-story stone building in an area of town as foreign to Hellie as Harry's Timbuktu. Orderly trees lined the manicured
street, and there were rows of identical buildings with identical stone
stairs spilling onto the clean, uncluttered street.

"This is it," the cabbie said, looking down to Hellie.

"What's it called again?" she asked, noticing the large sign above the
building's door.

"Society for Friendless Children," the cabbie read.

Hellie steeled her feelings, clenched her jaw to keep from crying.
The cab bounced gaily as the cabbie jumped down and opened the
door. "Need help with your valise?"

"Don't need help," she said, clutching the valise with everything she
owned to her chest. The building seemed to loom over her. She could
see several curious young faces looking out from the windows above.
Friendless children, she figured. "You *sure* this is the place?"

The cabbie climbed back into his seat and replied, "This is the place.
You go on in. They'll be good to you here."

She stood on the walk and watched the cabbie drive away. For a
brief moment the only sound on the street was the fading clop clop
clop of the horse's hooves. When they had faded entirely, Hellie turned
and went up the steps.

The front entrance door was unlocked, and Hellie slowly pushed the door open, feeling a gush of cool air as she did. The entry hall was empty of both adornment and persons.

"Hello?" she called out in a small voice.

She gingerly stepped toward the first door, which was half open. She peeped around it and saw it was being held open by a basket. Inside the basket was a sleeping baby.

"May I help you?" a man asked from inside the room.

"I . . . I . . ." she cleared her throat, then handed him the tattered flier. "I want to go west."

"I see," he said, looking at it.

"My brother Harry set it all up for today."

"Harry?"

"Harry Jondoe, 'cept he might have said Smith. Harry Smith." Just mentioning his name made her eyes sting, but no one sees Hellie Jondoe cry.

"Oh yes, I remember him." He shuffled through some papers on his desk, extracted one and said, "Yes, yes, here it is." He looked at her over his glasses. "He said there was a sister. Helena Smith."

Hellie took off her cap, rustled her hair, and said, "That's me, but let's get something straight: I'm Hellie Jondoe."

"All right. I'm Mr. Whitaker." He looked around. "But isn't Harry here to . . . ?"

"Harry's dead."

"What? You mean . . . how?"

"I ain't talking about it. Dead's dead."

He took off his reading glasses and looked Hellie over carefully. "Yes, I suppose so. And it says here in your paperwork there's no record of either of your parents. No guardian? Birth certificates? Parents' death certificates?"

"If you need a paper saying if you're dead or alive, then I reckon you're dead," Hellie said, looking out the window.

He smiled uneasily at this strange creature and said, "Well, we won't worry about all this. I have your brother's signature. The important thing is to get you a new start. A new family, you poor thing."

"I got a mark, if you need me to put it on something."

"You don't read or write?" he asked.

"If I could do one, I could do the other. Harry learned some reading. A lot of good it did him. I tried school a few times, but it didn't take. So Harry taught me some ABCs. Do I got to read to go west?"

"No, not at all. Many of our children are ignorant," he said.

"I ain't ignorant. I just can't read," she said, staring coolly at him. "So it's all set? I'm on that train today, right?"

"Oh yes, yes. Why don't you sit down? I'll get us some refreshment."

"Could use me a beer."

"I'll bet you could," he said, half to himself. "Well, we don't drink beer in this establishment."

She stepped carefully around the sleeping baby and sat down.

"I'll be right back," the man said.

Hellie looked around the room. Never had she seen so many photographs . . . all of children in neat, sad little groups, with a train in the background. She picked one off the desk and studied the little orphan faces, each with a wide-eyed, almost startled expression.

The baby started to fuss, and she looked down at it. The murmurs quickly escalated into a full-throttled howl, and Hellie got up, looked down, and ordered, "Shush!" She looked outside and down the hall but saw no one. Looking back down at the baby, she said, "Don't cry. Crying don't fix nothing, you'll learn that pretty damn quick." She moved the basket with her foot so it rocked a little, but that did nothing to soothe the wailing infant. In fact, the baby cried even louder, its face now red and wet and mad as sin . . . as though it knew someone was there and demanded to be attended to.

Finally, Hellie picked the baby up, held it at arm's length, and clumsily bounced it to settle its wriggling infant rage. "Now just pipe down," she said, unsure of what to do next. She brought it to her chest to cradle it, but that seemed to enrage the infant even more.

Then, on the desk, she saw the bottle, and she knew to pop the nipple into the baby's mouth. The baby clamored for the milk and started to pull at the nipple, gurgling with eagerness. Hellie sat back down carefully and watched the baby in her arms with both amazement and wonder at how quickly the child quieted and how eagerly it went for the bottle.

She looked at the child and noticed it seemed lopsided in her arms. She carefully lifted the blanket that enveloped it and winced as she saw the child had a deformed foot.

Just then, the man returned with a woman, dressed very much like a nurse, carrying a tray with a silver pot, two cups, and a plate of cookies.

"I see you've met Joey," the man said. The woman set the tray down on the table and looked at Hellie with that familiar glare of pity and disgust.

"This is my wife, Mrs. Whitaker."

"What happened to his leg?"

"Born that way. It's called a clubfoot. He'll always be a cripple," Mrs. Whitaker explained with a chilly snap. "Here, let me take him. He probably needs changing."

Hellie awkwardly surrendered the baby and the bottle, and Mrs. Whitaker left the room.

"How do you take your coffee?"

"Milk. Lots of sugar." He poured and handed it to Hellie, who downed it.

From the hall outside, Mrs. Whitaker called, "Jeb? Would you come here, please?"

"Yes, my dear." Then to Hellie as he left the room, "I'll be right back."

Hellie knew they were talking about her when she heard their low whispers, and she leaned toward the door to eavesdrop.

"Oh Jeb, she's more boy than girl. That hair! She's dark and dirty and smells like she lives on a garbage scow."

"Well, Martha, we'll just have to clean her up the best we can. But, she's a perfect age. Seems strong. Can't read, though."

"Oh great. That's another strike against her."

"Don't worry, don't worry. You know Miss Bergeson places every child we send out."

"Oh yeah? What about Lizzie?" Mrs. Whitaker reminded him flatly.

"Well, okay, there *is* Lizzie. But she's not coming back this time. I already set it up with Miss Bergeson."

"How? Who wants to spend their life looking at Lizzie? *I* could barely look at her these last six months," she said.

"Miss Bergeson is going to insist Lizzie and Joey stay together," he said. "That way, the cripple has a full-time caretaker. We'll kill two birds with one stone. So, I say we get our little guttersnipe on today's train and be grateful for the profit."

"All right, Jeb, but that's the last time you pay fifty dollars for a brat sight unseen."

Hellie stepped away from the door, the sting of betrayal replacing her fear and her grief. Fifty dollars.

"We taking in hoboes now?" the girl, about Hellie's age, asked from the top of the stairs, giving Hellie a snippy little up-and-down glance.

"Lizzie, you're a fine one to throw stones," Mrs. Whitaker said, as she led Hellie up the staircase to the third floor.

Hellie looked at the girl and noticed half her face was sagging, as though her head was made of bread dough that some joker punched half down, then baked that way. A closer look and Hellie could see networks of broken vessels and scars surrounding a sagging, lifeless, half-closed eye.

At the top of the landing, Mrs. Whitaker said, "Lizzie, this is Helena, our new girl."

"That's a girl?"

If they had been on the streets, she would have returned the girl's remark with something twice as evil with the accompaniment of a well-aimed horse turd in her slingshot.

"Dry up," Hellie growled back.

Mrs. Whitaker opened a cupboard and pulled out two towels and a robe.

"What's in your hobo pack?" Lizzie continued. "Bet you don't even own a dress."

She pulled at the valise, but Hellie tugged it back and said, "Drop dead, you little . . ."

"*Ladies*," Mrs. Whitaker warned.

"My mother made sure I had five dresses when she brought me here," Lizzie trumped, following them to the girls' showers.

"Your *mother* brought you here?" Hellie asked. "Ain't this a orphanage?" Hellie noticed Lizzie had a small rag doll tucked into the back of her skirt, just the way she tucked away Slim in her pants belt. To each her own security, she thought.

"She was sick and dying of a horrible disease, so she brought me here," Lizzie said. "So I didn't have to watch her die."

"What a good sport," Hellie said.

"Lizzie," Mrs. Whitaker said, "I have told you and told you, it's not a child's past we're concerned with, it's a child's future. Helena, go take a shower and leave your clothes where they fall. Put on that robe and then you can rest up on that bed at the very end of the dormitory. You look exhausted." She pointed to the long room across the hall.

"Only babies take naps," Lizzie snipped as Hellie took the towels and robe and looked into the showers.

"Lizzie," Mrs. Whitaker said, "are you all packed?"

"No! I told you I don't want to go again! I want to stay here and be a nun."

"My dear, you have to be Catholic to be a nun. Your family was Methodist."

"I don't care! I don't want to go."

Mrs. Whitaker looked at Hellie and said, "Go ahead. Shower and a nap. I'll wake you when it's time to leave." She took Lizzie's arm and said, "Now, Lizzie, let's you and me have a little talk."

"Ow! Let go!"

Hellie had no idea where the other orphan girls were, but she was grateful she had the showers to herself. She turned on all the showers, the sink faucets, and then flushed all the toilets, pulling on the chains with angry jerks. She shed her clothes, stood in the middle of the showers, and, with the rush of water to cover her voice, let out a scream of anguish. With the shower to disguise her tears, she leaned against the shower wall and let the water cascade over her.

When she emerged, her old clothes had vanished, and she wrapped herself in the robe and made her way to the dormitory, where she put her valise into the bed and climbed in next to it and was instantly asleep.

When she startled awake several hours later, she found Lizzie sitting on the next bed over, watching her like a cat watches a fledgling leave the nest. Hellie quickly made sure her valise was still next to her. "What are you looking at?"

"You. Mrs. Whitaker says you're a charity case, so I have to be nice to you," she stated.

"Ain't everyone here a charity case?" Hellie said, sitting on the bed.

"And she said since I've been out before, I have to help you."

"I don't need any help . . . what do you mean, been out before? Out where?"

"Been out west. On the train. Looking for a home," Lizzie explained. "This will be my third time. The first time I still had bandages, the second time I cried the whole time. No one wants a bandaged, crying, half-blind girl, so I came back. Mrs. Whitaker was fit to be tied! She doesn't get the two hundred smackers unless they find you a home."

"Don't worry. I ain't coming back."

"I don't want to be adopted," Lizzie said. "I want to stay here and be a nun."

"Suit yourself," Hellie said. "I gotta shake hands with Miss Pisser."

Lizzie gasped and put her hand to her mouth. "That's not nice!"

Hellie took her valise and said, "You ain't heard nothing yet."

When she returned, Lizzie was sitting atop Hellie's bed. Slim the slingshot was in her lap.

"Hey! Gimme that!" Hellie said.

Lizzie stood on the bed and held it higher. "No, I found it! It's mine!"

"You stole it! Where did you find it?"

"It was in your bed. Finders keepers, losers weepers!" Lizzie said. While she jumped, her doll fell out of her skirt. Hellie quickly snatched it up and held it as hostage out the window.

"Gimme my slingshot or I toss this out!"

"No! You give me my Mary back!"

The racket brought Mrs. Whitaker and several curious children to the door.

"Just what is going on here?" she demanded.

The girls spoke over each other, explaining their outrage.

"Lizzie, you are too old for dolls," Mrs. Whitaker said, demanding the doll from Hellie. "And you, young lady!" she said, taking the slingshot from Lizzie and pointing it at Hellie. "Young ladies do not use slingshots."

"You can't take that!" Hellie said, approaching the woman with clenched fists.

"I can and I will," she said. She took a key from her pocket, showed it to them, then unlocked a closet at the end of the dormitory. She placed the doll and the slingshot on the shelf, locked the door, and said, "Lizzie, please go help downstairs. And you, Helena Smith . . ."

"Hellie Jondoe!"

"I don't suppose you have anything decent to wear in that valise of yours?"

11

"*Well, you* **have** *to wear it.* Girls dress like girls," Mrs. Whitaker said, holding up the wrinkled skirt she'd taken out of Hellie's valise. "This skirt, that blouse, and I suppose we can get by with that, even though it's a boy's jacket. We'll hang it outside the train window to air it out." She picked up the straw hat, which had been crushed at the bottom of the valise, and examined the creased brim and frayed blue ribbon. "This will have to do, too. Our storeroom is bare."

Hellie's face scowled. "Skirts ain't useful," she said.

"They are if you're trying to find a home," Mrs. Whitaker said, almost under her breath. She looked at Hellie's freshly bobbed hair and said, "And what happened to your hair?"

"Got it caught in a weaving machine," she said, taking the skirt from her.

"Well, it will grow, thank heaven. A young lady's crowning glory is her hair, you know. And hurry. We all have to be out that front door and in the wagon by three sharp." She indicated the large clock on the wall of the dormitory room.

Hellie looked at it, then back to Mrs. Whitaker, who made a face and said, "When the big hand is . . ."

"I can tell time," Hellie said. "I ain't *totally* ignorant." She was struggling with the buttons on her skirt. "How's this go?"

"Oh here, let me," Mrs. Whitaker said impatiently, yanking the skirt around so the button was in the back. Then she scurried off down the hall toward the nursery.

Hellie looked at herself in the mirror, feeling the odd coolness of air between her bare legs and the scratchiness of the underskirt. She lifted the skirt to inspect her pencil-thin legs and knobby, scarred knees. She popped the lopsided straw hat on and thought she looked like a dim-witted uptown girl. She gave it an expert fling, and it spun and floated, the ribbon like a kite's tail, right out the window. She took her cap out of the valise and cocked it on her head.

Before leaving the room, she extracted the key she had easily lifted from Mrs. Whitaker when she was helping her with the skirt button. She walked to the storage closet, unlocked it, and went in, having no intention of going anywhere without Slim. Next to a kite, a wooden boat, and other childhood comforts and left-behinds sat Lizzie's precious rag doll. Next to it was Slim. She tucked the slingshot into the long pocket at the side of her skirt and took Lizzie's doll, three balls, a handful of lead soldiers, tops, and marbles and dropped them in her valise. She snapped it shut, relocked the door, pocketed the key, and went downstairs.

The hall was filled with children sitting along the corridor: girls on the right, boys on the left. How could so many children be so still and quiet and well-mannered? There must have been forty or more, ranging in age from seven-month-old Joey to Lizzie, almost grown. She took her place at the end of the line of girls, tossed down her valise, and plopped down next to Lizzie.

"I don't like you," Lizzie said in a low whisper.

"You started it."

"My mother made me that doll."

"I made me that slingshot," Hellie said back.

Mrs. Whitaker came into the hall. Children moved their legs to let her pass. She stopped and looked down at Hellie. "Where's your boater? You look horrible in that newsboy cap. Give it to me."

"No."

The woman's hand swooped down and snatched the cap off Hellie's head. "Learning to do as you are told is the first step toward a new and better life, young lady."

The eyes of all the children were on her, bringing Hellie to simmering rage. Mrs. Whitaker proceeded to make each child stand up and turn around for her inspection.

"All right," she announced. "Children, I want silent prayer until the wagon comes around."

The heads went obediently down. Even the toddlers bowed their heads.

"What the hell are we praying for?" Hellie asked Mrs. Whitaker.

"Homes, of course. Although you might pray for a civil tongue."

She left. After a half hour of this unnatural silence, the heat from the hallway was starting to build. Hellie could tell the children were trying to keep to their prayers, but they were starting to fidget.

She quietly opened her valise, took out a ball, and rolled it across the hall, where it landed between the legs of a young boy. He looked at it, then at Hellie. Hellie put her finger to her lips. The boy grabbed the ball and pocketed it, his face alive with thanks.

She did the same thing with other little toys she had stolen from the closet, until the kids were each grinning and sending silent thank yous over to their new benefactor.

Finally, she looked at Lizzie. Slowly, she pulled just the head of the doll, Mary, out of her valise. The side of Lizzie's face that worked lit up, and Hellie could tell that at least half of the girl was quite pretty.

"You promise to not never take nothing of mine again?" Hellie asked.

Lizzie looked at her. "I promise."

At that, Hellie gave Lizzie her precious Mary, which was quickly pocketed.

Lizzie offered her hand. "Elizabeth. Call me Lizzie."

"Hellie. Call me Hellie." She took her hand and they shook.

"Hell's bells, even your name's a swear word," Lizzie giggled.

Mr. and Mrs. Whitaker came in the front door and announced the wagon had at last arrived. Each child grinned with their stolen treasure secreted away.

Two lines of children, each toting a valise or case, marched out the front doors, down the steps, and piled two by two into the large wagon. Even Hellie had to admit to a certain excitement.

When they were seated in the wagon, Lizzie asked, "How did you get all those toys?"

"I'm a thief." She extracted the large skeleton key to the dormitory closet and placed it in the pouch of her slingshot. Taking aim, she let the key fly. The tinkling of glass as the key shattered a windowpane brought a satisfied grin to each girl's face.

Lizzie reached into her pocket and pulled out a lint-covered jawbreaker. "Here," she said, "Do one for me."

12

Hellie had worked Grand Central Station plenty of times. Nothing like a hurried, excited crowd to spy a mark and flimp a pocket or two. She knew every corner, pillar, bench, and gate around which a cop was likely to hide and watched carefully as the wagon deposited them on the great sidewalk outside the main entrance. "Now listen, children," Mr. Whitaker said over the bobbing orphan heads. "It's important we all stay together. You older children take the hand of a younger child." This was standard procedure, and each child seem to have a favorite hand to grip, leaving Hellie without one. Mrs. Whitaker placed baby Joey in her arms. Just as well, Hellie thought. She could feel her fingers itch with the possibilities a well-adorned woman, distracted by the orphans, presented.

"Now, you will have a whole train car all to yourselves, boys and girls," Mr. Whitaker went on. "But you must be very, very good and very, very quiet. Ladies and gentlemen are what the railroad company expects out of you, and that is what they shall have for allowing you to ride for free."

Hellie turned to Lizzie and said, "Sounds like he ain't going."

"He never goes. He stays here and finds more orphans. *She'll* be going with us," she said, indicating a stony-faced, tall, thin woman dressed in black from head to toe. "That's Miss Bergeson. She's the one who takes us out west."

"Children! Children!" Mr. Whitaker called, gathering them toward him. "This is Miss Bergeson. And this is Mr. Evans. They are going to take over from here. Now I want you to show them every kindness and courtesy you would show myself and Mrs. Whitaker. Miss Bergeson knows what's best for you all, and I want you do exactly as she says. She'll be your guardian every step of your journey. Now, one last prayer before you get on the train."

The children instinctively bowed their heads. "Miss Bergeson, will you do the honors?"

"Dear heavenly father, please look down on these the most needy of all your unfortunate. Help us on our journey to find a home for each and every child. Even those whom you have seen fit to burden with poverty and imperfect bodies and minds."

Hellie wasn't praying. By habit, she never took her eyes off a crowd.

"And teach us to accept our lots in life and to know Thy will be done," Miss Bergeson concluded. "We ask it in the name of our Lord, our savior and our only hope for salvation, amen."

At that, Mr. Evans, a small, thin, graying man, took charge of the boys while Miss Bergeson took Hellie aside and said, "Which one are you?"

"Hellie Jondoe."

She consulted a roster of names and said, "Oh, yes. Helena Smith. The street urchin, fresh off the rocky path. Looks like we got you just in time. Martha Whitaker warned me about you. Now let me warn *you*, young lady, I demand obedience. You will do exactly as I say every step of this journey, and you will pray to God above that He finds you worthy enough to be taken in by some Christian family."

Her eyes landed on Lizzie. A thin smile came across her lips. "And Lizzie," she seemed to sing. "I will pray the third time's the charm for you. Wouldn't hurt you to do a little more praying, either."

The woman inspected Joey in Hellie's arms. "Oh yes. The cripple baby. What's his name? Joey. Give Joey to Lizzie. From now on, he is your responsibility, Lizzie."

"But . . ."

"*Your* responsibility," she repeated.

She walked off to take leadership of the group.

"Bergie's a witch," Lizzie whispered.

"Hand in hand, follow me, children," their keeper commanded.

Hellie looked at Lizzie and said, "Witches don't scare me none."

The train had already been loaded with cargo and the regular passengers. They were led to their car far toward the end of the train, past the Pullmans, sleepers, and dining and baggage cars and just before the freight cars.

Waiting for them on the platform was another woman. This one was dressed in a sturdy tan dress, boots, and a vest. She wore her hair high on her head, but it seemed hastily fashioned and held haphazardly with pins and combs and a pencil that all stuck out at odd angles. A black lock had escaped and bounced carefree along the side of her face, to be blown or absently swiped away as the woman worked.

She had several open cases around her, and she was making some adjustments to a large camera set upon a tripod. When she saw Miss Bergeson leading the pack of hand-holding children, she walked briskly over to her.

"Hello. Are you Miss Bergeron?" she asked.

"Bergeson," she corrected with a chilly smile.

"Oh, yes. I'm here to take the photographs," she said, indicating the awaiting tripod. "I believe Jeb Whitaker arranged it."

"Yes, we always get a departure picture, but a *woman* photographer? Nobody said anything to me about a *woman* photographer," Miss Bergeson said, her voice full of disapproval.

"It doesn't take the strength of a man to push a little shutter button," the photographer replied, smiling through full red lips and a set of perfect white teeth.

"Very well. All right, children," Miss Bergeson said, clapping her hands to get everyone's attention. "Everyone line up, taller children in the back, smaller in front."

"Look," Lizzie whispered in Hellie's ear. "She's wearing lip paint."

Of course, lip paint was nothing new to Hellie's eyes, nor as scandalous.

"Aren't her eyes beautiful?" Hellie said back. "All catlike." She pulled the corners of her eyes back and asked, "Do I look like her?"

"Hurry!" Miss Bergeson said, pulling both girls by the sleeves and placing them in the back row. Just as the photographer had set up for the photograph, Joey began to cry. Miss Bergeson said to Lizzie, "Lizzie, take that baby over there. Nobody wants a photograph of a screaming baby."

"No, that's all right," the photographer said.

"Do as you're told!" Miss Bergeson said. Lizzie got out of line and took the screaming child away.

There was a huge flash and pop, followed by surprised expressions on the faces of the children and a greenish smoke and an acrid smell from the chemicals that ignited the flash. Joey wailed even louder.

"You have your photograph," Miss Bergeson said, clapping her hands to route the children toward the train. "All right children, two by two."

Hellie waited for Lizzie. "I never got my picture tooken before. I wonder how our faces get from here to on the paper."

Lizzie said, sticking her thumb into Joey's mouth for him to suck. "Bergie always finds a reason to leave me out of the going-away photographs. She probably thinks a face like mine will break the camera. Then nobody's faces get from here to on the paper."

Hellie looked at her, saw Lizzie's odd, crooked smile, and gave her a slow, kindred smile back.

They boarded the train. Miss Bergeson assigned Hellie and Lizzie seats at the back of the car. Joey had fallen asleep in Lizzie's arms. Hellie looked around the platform as the lady photographer gathered up her supplies and hurriedly dashed down the platform, hardly hobbled at all by her long hobble skirt. And her boots had those high heels, Hellie noticed. How could she move so fast and gracefully dressed like that and with each arm hauling a large case? Hellie opened the window and watched her get into the train just two cars ahead of them.

She nudged Lizzie next to her, who was daring a peek at her doll hidden in the folds of her skirt. "That lady making the pictures is getting on the train."

Lizzie shrugged and said, "Maybe she's an orphan."

Mr. and Mrs. Whitaker appeared at the front of the car, bidding farewell to each child and handing them a piece of candy and a Bible. When she got to the last seat, she said. "And Lizzie, I know you already have your Bible, but pass this to Hellie, will you?"

Hellie took the candy cane out of the center of the Bible and handed the book back. "You can have this back," she said. "I'll keep the candy."

Miss Bergeson had appeared next to Mrs. Whitaker. "No, you keep that Bible," Miss Bergeson said.

"I don't *need* that Bible. Can't read it anyhows."

"Well, maybe you should just think about the Lord's word until you *can* read," Mrs. Whitaker snapped. She dropped the Bible on her lap.

All eyes were on them. Lizzie seemed to shrink into her seat, rocking Joey. Hellie picked up the Bible and held it out. "I got better things to think about." Then she dropped the Bible onto the floor.

The conductor stuck his head into the car and announced they were ready to pull out. Mrs. Whitaker glared at Hellie and then said to Miss Bergeson, "Good luck, Miss Bergeson." She quickly left the train.

"Pick it up!" Miss Bergeson said down to Hellie.

The train lurched forward.

"Just do it," Lizzie whispered to her, quaking in Miss Bergeson's shadow.

Hellie picked it up.

"That's better," Miss Bergeson said with a small triumphant smile on her thin, pale lips. She went to the front of the car.

On the platform below, Hellie saw the Whitakers waving goodbye. Hellie called out her open window, "I don't need your damn Bible!" And she tossed it at them just as the train pulled out.

For her blasphemy, she spent the first night of the journey riding alone, without food, locked in the baggage car.

13

Hellie had built herself a hidey-hole among the luggage and the crates and the boxes going west, her own valise safely by her side. Hidey-holes were all she had known, a source of comfort and safety, even warmth. She pulled out her cash and counted it. She looked at the war poster of the drowned mother and child and found it oddly peaceful. Then she examined the photos of her mother, now with a stab through the middle, and stared at the faces . . . the young girl, the fully grown woman. She saw Harry in the eyes; she saw herself in the faint smile.

Then, with the photos in one hand, the wad of bills in the other, she felt tears filling her eyes—slow and tentative at first, then building until impossible to hold in. Down her cheeks to drip off her shaking chin. For once, it felt good not to dash or damn the tears away . . . to let them gush—without witnesses, without rage. As though each tear gave courage to the next, she was soon sobbing aloud, the gentle, reliable ca-click, ca-click of the tracks beneath her the only reply.

How many miles did she cry? How much farther away was she now? Could a girl cry all the way to Timbuktu or wherever she was heading? She tried to relax and reach for even breaths, but her chest kept grasping for air with shaky breaths. *Can a person die from crying,* she wondered.

"Stop it, Hellie! Ain't doing no one no good!" she finally said.

The lock in the baggage compartment door clicked. She watched the shadow of a person through the frosted glass window. Dashing her sleeve across her face, she hunkered down low.

The intruder entered and was rummaging through luggage, mutter-ing. "Oh, rats to the Kaiser, where *are* those . . . ?"

Hellie ventured a peek over a stack of suitcases and saw it was the photographer woman, now half-swallowed by a huge steamer trunk. She finally stood up with a small box. She smiled as she opened it and extracted a cigarette. She sat on her trunk, struck a match along the side, lit the cigarette, and inhaled a long draw. Hellie could hear the photographer's satisfied sigh as she exhaled the smoke.

"I can see you, you know," the woman stated.

Slowly, Hellie's head came up.

The woman fanned the smoke and smiled as she looked at Hellie. "Oh. You're one of the orphans."

"Ain't a orphan. I'm just hitching a ride west," Hellie stated. Then, "That's between you and me, okay? You won't tell that Miss Bergeson in there, will you?" She nodded her head toward the orphan car behind them.

"That horse's ass? I wouldn't tell her if her hair was on fire."

Hellie laughed ever so slightly at the vision of Miss Bergeson streak-ing through the train cars, trying to outrun her long, flaming locks.

The photographer looked at Hellie's tear-streaked, blotchy red face and swollen eyes. "Looks like you needed that laugh."

Hellie wiped her face again and said, "You woke me up, that's all."

"Smoke?"

"I quit."

"Uh huh." Her eyes landed on the photograph of Hellie's mother, which had slipped to the floor. "May I?" She looked at the photograph, examining the pose, the lighting, the studio's mark. "A beautiful photo-graph. Your mother?"

"That's what Harry, my brother, tells—told me," she replied, reach-ing for the photograph. She felt the burn of new tears at the mention of his name, but was quick to recover.

"Is Harry one of the other orph . . . not orphans on the train?"

"He ain't nothing no more 'cept dead," she stated with the "that's that" view of death she'd learned so well on the streets of the Bowery.

"Oh. I'm sorry."

Hellie looked at the photo and said wistfully, "Wish I had a picture of him now, too. These come in handy once someone's dead, don't they? Like they're all froze up in time."

The photographer smiled vaguely and repeated, "Froze up in time. Hmm. Always young and beautiful. Yes, photographs do come in handy. I never thought of it that way."

Hellie sniffed and ran her sleeve under her nose again. The woman handed her a lavender-scented hankie. Hellie used it to blow her nose, then offered it back.

"No. Keep it. I have dozens. Really."

"Harry says we don't take charity."

The photographer took back her hankie. "Very well." She dashed her cigarette out on the floor and asked, "So, what did you do to end up locked in here?"

"Blastemy or something," she said. "Whatever she called it, ain't gonna show up on my list of sins."

"List of sins? Someone of your tender years has a list of sins? Perhaps picking apples off your neighbor's tree? Sneaking a candy at the drugstore?"

Hellie looked at the woman and found something odd in her voice. Sarcasm? Sympathy? "Assault, robbery . . . murder maybe," she said, carefully watching the woman's reaction. Their eyes met across the car. "Self-defense murder," Hellie amended with a shaky conviction. A pause. Then she added in a low, quavering whisper, "Him-or-me murder." She raised her head and added, "So blastemy ain't no big concern to me."

There was a brief silence as they eyed each other. Finally, the photographer said, "No, I suppose 'blastemy' ain't too high on your list of sins."

"So, why you heading west?" Hellie asked.

The woman reached into a pocket and pulled out a card. She handed it to Hellie, whose face reddened as she looked at it. The photographer recognized her embarrassment, took back the card, and read, "A.B.E. Collier, Photographer-Journalist. Then it has my address and telephone number."

"You keep a card to remember it?" Hellie asked.

The woman laughed and said, "No, this is a business card. It's for drumming up business."

"So does that work?" Hellie asked.

"Well," she admitted, pinning a lock of hair back up, "when clients find out A.B.E. stands for Amanda Beulah Emmaline, they usually break for the hills. You saw Miss Bergeson's reaction back there at Grand Central." She took a camera out of the trunk and began to clean the lens and added, "Men's reactions are usually even worse. Seems women are too *fra-gile* to chronicle history. Don't let my name scare you. Call me Amanda. What do I call you?"

"Hellie Jondoe," Hellie replied, oddly comfortable in the company of this young woman.

"John Doe? As in 'I-don't-know-my-last-name?'" she asked, sitting on a trunk. "Wouldn't that be Jane Doe?"

"I don't know about her. I'm Hellie Jondoe and I'll fight the man or woman who says I ain't."

"I'll bet you would," Amanda said, a smile of appreciation coming to her lips.

"So, there much money taking photographs out west?" Hellie asked, pointing to the business card on the trunk between them.

"I hope so. I intend to write a story about the orphan trains and sell it with my pictures. Oh, and don't tell the horse's ass, okay? I'm calling it 'A Journey Home.' I'm going to see if Mr. Hearst, oh, you probably wouldn't know about him . . . anyway, I want to sell the story to his newspapers."

"What for? I mean, what do folks care about orphans and trains?" Hellie asked.

Miss Collier looked at her camera. "Nothing. And that's the problem. People don't give one iota. Just get the orphans out of the city. Give them to the farmers. Let them take society's mistakes and waifs. Good farmhands and cleaning girls are hard to find."

"Well, I ain't being no farmhand," Hellie said. "Can I?" she asked, picking up the camera.

"Go ahead. Look through the lens. Right there. See me?"

"Yeah, but you're sitting on your head," Hellie said.

"That's the way it's supposed to be."

Hellie kept looking around the baggage car through the lens. "So, how come you know all this orphan train business?"

The photographer smiled into the lens now trained on her and replied, "Because seventeen years ago, I was sent out on an orphan train. Ended up with a family in Kansas. Six years of living hell. So, now I'm going to tell the story for the world to read. We call it an 'exposé' in the journalism business. You know, Hellie Jondoe, now that we've shared a few secrets, maybe we're comrades in arms."

Always suspicious, Hellie's face darkened. "I ain't totin'."

Miss Collier's face went blank. Then she burst into a most unladylike, contagious howl, bringing a smile to Hellie's face. "Well, neither am I." She pointed to the camera and added, "There. That's all I'm totin'. What I meant was maybe you can help with my story idea."

"How?"

"Just let me take your picture along the trip. And we can talk. Like this."

"And you can write it all up? What's in it for me?"

"What would you like?"

Hellie looked into the camera lens again. "I like looking in this thing and seeing the world upside down. Kind of like the way I see things anyhow. How's about you could show me how it all works?"

Amanda Beulah Emmaline Collier smiled broadly at Hellie. "Deal. Want to shake on it?" She offered her hand across the trunk.

Hellie shook it and said, "Deal."

"Now, children," *Miss Bergeson called* from the front of the orphan car. The train had pulled into the first orphan stop, Canton, Ohio, and each nose was plastered to a window. "Please!" After two days in the train, the children had been conditioned to respond to the alto timbre of Bergeson's voice when she bellowed "please!" The heads snapped around, and their attention was on Miss Bergeson and Mr. Evans standing next to her. The journey thus far had been dotted with stops and train changes, but the children were not allowed off the train except in guarded twos and then only to get fresh air and to stretch their restless legs. Miss Bergeson had found a reason to keep both Hellie and Lizzie on the train at every stop.

But not this one.

"There's A.B.E. Collier," Hellie said, pointing out the photographer, who was the first one off her car and scurrying along with her cases of photography equipment.

"What's she doing?"

"She's going to take our pictures some more," Hellie said. "She's doing—what'd she call it? Exposer or something."

"Why?"

"Elizabeth Coultrane! Helena Smith!" Miss Bergeson shouted. The other orphans, each now dressed in their best clothes, turned to look at them and hushed them, since the rule was that no one did or got anything until *all* eyes were on Bergeson.

"Thank you," she said. "Now, we will walk, two by two, across the street, and you will follow me into the . . ." She paused while Mr. Evans pointed out something to her on a clipboard. "Follow me to the Pioneer Schoolhouse. Now, remember, not all of you will find a home today. In fact, most of you will not. We have many more stops to make across country, so do not lose heart. God will provide as God sees fit."

"Think God could see fit to provide us a steak dinner?" Hellie asked Lizzie out of the corner of her mouth. Lizzie jabbed her.

"We shall sing 'Onward, Christian Soldiers' as we march to the schoolhouse. You older children must sing extra, extra loud. Heads held high. Voices proud. Remember, these fine people will be looking for good, Christian children to bring into their families. First impressions are very important. Only speak when you are spoken to. You Bradley children," her gaze settled on the four Bradleys—two boys, two girls, huddled together, ages like clockwork, four, six, eight, and ten. "I do not want you sitting together."

"Why?" Hellie asked Lizzie.

"You'll see," she whispered back.

They made a curious sight—the children, two by two, some gaily skipping, some, like little Joey, being carried, others fearful and crying, limping their way through "Onward, Christian Soldiers," the voices of Bergeson at the front and Evans at the rear, booming loudest.

Onlookers from the train and the streets stood to watch the parade and let the children pass. Some followed them down the street toward the Pioneer Schoolhouse.

Hellie looked around the town. "So, this is the hicks," she said. "Look how much sky you can see."

"Well, of course you can see sky," Lizzie said.

"Not where I come from," Hellie said. "Bet there's not one decent hidey-hole in this whole town."

"Ladies, please," Mr. Evans said from behind them. "Keep up."

The group stopped at the foot of the steps leading to the schoolhouse. A banner had been erected, and it flapped as though waving a limp welcome in the June breeze.

"What's it say?" Hellie asked Lizzie, who was scrunching her one good eye up at it.

"Wel-come, or-phans," she said, sounding out the syllables carefully.

Amanda had her camera set up and was on the sidewalk taking photographs of the group as they arrived. She had a smaller camera swinging from a leather strap around her neck.

"Who told you you could take all these photographs?" Miss Bergeson said, pointing a long finger at the camera.

"It's a free country."

"We'll see about that!" she snapped.

"Smile!" the photographer said, taking a photograph of her— openmouthed and red-faced—using the box camera hanging from her neck.

"Miss Bergeson?" a man, nicely dressed and with a carnation in his lapel, asked from the top of the steps.

"Yes?"

"I'm Samuel Winters, the mayor of Canton. Your Mr. Whitaker called this morning to make sure everything was ready. Please, won't you bring the children inside? Some ladies from the Congregational Church have prepared a little reception. Oh, I see you have a little one. We'll arrange to have a bottle warmed."

"Wonderful," she gushed, whisking Joey out of Lizzie's arms.

"We wanted to wait until the folks from the outer farms got here before beginning. I hope the children don't mind waiting."

Miss Bergeson fingered the gold cross around her neck and said, "Our precious children have waited all their lives for this opportunity, Mr. Winters. I'm sure they can wait a little bit longer." She turned on the steps and called out, "Children! Two by two."

Hellie stopped with Lizzie at the foot of the steps and posed for a photograph.

"Thank you, girls," Amanda said, with a smile and a wink.

Hellie paused before going up the steps.

"What?" Lizzie asked.

"Ain't never been inside a school before."

"Well, don't worry. Nobody's going to make you learn anything," Lizzie said, holding out her hand. "Come on. Two by two."

Hellie ignored her offering and walked past her up the steps.

They were ushered into a large room with a small stage at one end. On the stage, in two neat rows of twenty, were small chairs for the children. A large table with several adult chairs was set up at the base of the stage. There were stacks of papers on top.

Miss Bergeson was introduced to the other people waiting there.

"And this is Dr. Harrison, our community health doctor, Dr. Insley, dentist in the same capacity. This is Reverend Overby, the chairman of our search committee. Mrs. Elliott has been handling publicity. You know, getting word out to the community and the newspapers."

He rubbed his hands together genially, looking over the children who were being seated on the stage.

If nervous, childlike excitement could be grabbed from the air, Hellie could have seized herself an armful.

15

The first people to enter the room, wearing their tired, workaday clothes, weren't dressed much better than the orphans. They came in slowly and seemingly shy at first. Then, as though drawing on the courage of the previous person, folks entered, made a name tag, pinned it on, and eventually found seats. The room quickly filled with a steamy sense of excitement, mixing smells of freshly plowed dirt and the sweat that accompanies it, hastily splashed rose water, and scorched coffee.

Each child was given a card on a string that was placed around his or her neck announcing to those gathered a name and an age. Then, each was handed a glass of milk and a cookie, but when Hellie asked for a cold beer instead, she was quickly rebuked and told to just sit and eat her cookie. She caught the eye of a thin, drab woman as she passed in front of the stage, inspecting each child as she passed. She pulled her husband's sleeve and whispered something to him, indicating a child. Hellie looked down the row and saw she was looking at the little blonde toddler called Emily. She was a pretty little child and no doubt would be the first child snatched off the stage and into a new life, like the cutest, plumpest puppy is the pick of the litter. Who could turn down a sweet, little, curly-headed blonde? Hellie thought. Never mind the brat coughed all night long, wet the bed, and whined constantly for her mother.

The couple passed, got some coffee, and took their seat as Mayor Winters took the stage and called for everyone's attention. The minister was asked to give a prayer. Hellie didn't bow her head, or listen, but rather watched the people in front of her. She tried to mentally pair up the children with the families. The strong young boys with the farmers, the smart young girls with the shopkeepers, the babies with the dry old people hoping finally for a child of their very own or a replacement for one resting under sod.

Hellie flashed on a vision of Harry. This humiliation, this display, was all his fault. He's messed everything up. She shook his face from her memory just as the folks said "amen," and the heads came up, eyes scanning the children on the stage.

One little boy, sitting between his parents, stared coolly up at Hellie, then stuck out a long, pink tongue, dotted with mashed cookie. Hellie shot him an obscene gesture. Lizzie watched the whole thing and did the same when it appeared no one was looking. His mouth dropped open, and he nudged his mother and pointed at them.

Just then, a flash from the back of the room startled the crowd. Folks turned around, and Amanda said, "Please, just go about your business. Don't mind me."

Miss Bergeson puffed with indignation and Lizzie and Hellie grinned.

Reverend Overby invited people to come up and talk to the children.

"But please, ladies and gentlemen, try not to ask about a child's past," Miss Bergeson added. "After all, it's the future of these lambs we are concerned about, not their painful pasts."

The room was alive with noise as people scooted chairs, mulled around, came on the stage, and started to talk to the children. Hellie and Lizzie quickly moved toward the back of the stage and hid among the black curtains while the younger children were surrounded by prospective parents. Bergeson and Evans cheerfully introduced some children who had been instructed to either curtsy or shake hands, smile big, stand straight, and always reply with a polite "ma'am" or "sir."

Soon, little groups formed as people took a child aside to sit and chat. Hellie and Lizzie stood together. Finally, a young boy, about their age, approached them from the stage. "Hey, Ma! There's some girls back here!" Then, he took a closer look at Lizzie and said, "Wow, your face is all . . ." He was at a loss for words. "All . . ." His words trailed off as he looked through the fork of Hellie's drawn slingshot.

"Evaporate, punk," Hellie warned.

"Okay," the boy answered. "Ma had her heart set on a little girl anyhows," he said, backing away. Then, he added, "One with a whole face, too!"

Hellie got him square between his shoulders. He yelped and went crying to his mother.

"Come on, Lizzie," Hellie said, pulling her between the curtains to the small backstage area.

"We can't just leave. Bergie will . . ."

"Oh, hang Bergie. She's busy out front. Come on. Let's you and me get us a soda. Got to be some soda pop somewhere in this hick town." They found the back door, but Lizzie pulled away as Hellie leaped down the steps, letting her skirts fly.

"Now what's wrong?" Hellie asked.

"You don't know Bergie the way I do. She'll whip us good for running away. Last time out Billie Jenkins ran off and he was nothing but black and blue when she got done with him. Had to tell the folks at the next stop he'd taken a spill off the luggage rack."

"We'll just say you had to find the outhouse and before you know it, things was over and we headed back to the train," Hellie explained.

Lizzie was halfway back inside the stage door and said, "No, Hellie. I'm going back."

"Cripes, from the sounds of it, you want to get yourself adopted. So much for the nun house, huh? So why you want to go back in there and get adopted?"

At this Lizzie laughed. "Hellsbells, no one is going to adopt *me*!" She pulled her long hair away from her damaged face as though to remind Hellie of her looks.

"Oh, yes, they are. I heard them Whitakers say you and Joey was both getting homes. *Together*. Bergie's fixing it. You're going to be a two-fer."

"A what?"

"You know. Two for the price of one. A two-fer. So if I was you, I wouldn't go back in there, if you want to go back to New York."

"You heard them say that?"

"I did. I figure that's why Bergie says Joey's your responsibility."

Lizzie looked crushed. Hellie said softly, "Lizzie, that ain't so bad. Joey's a real sweet baby. Heck, anyone gets either of you, gets a real bargain. And no matter what, you got yourself a brother. Now that I think about it, maybe you better go on in there. Not me, though. I'm riding that train as far as I can. I want as much territory between me and New York City as I can get. Ain't nothing left for me in New York."

"You two are in trouble!" a small voice warned through the back door.

Miss Bergeson glared at them as they reappeared between the stage curtains, then quickly smiled up at the couple who were in front of her. She indicated where they were to sign, and they walked away, each with a Bradley child, one boy, one girl, in hand. Screaming at the top of his lungs was James Bradley, being held back by Mr. Evans. "You promised we could stay together!"

The couple, hesitant, yet unyielding in their choices, were guided out of the building by Miss Bergeson.

Hellie felt a sense of rage. She looked at Lizzie.

"That's why she didn't want them sitting together," Lizzie explained. "You'll get used to it," she added, picking up a fussing Joey from his basket and rocking him to and fro.

Hellie looked then at James, who was now cradling his remaining sister and quieting her sobbing.

The childlike sense of excitement and joy that escorted the children in had vanished an hour later. The thirty-three rejected orphans who boarded the train, two by two, were quiet, sullen, and crying now . . . but only to themselves.

16

The remaining orphans now had a little more room to move about their railroad car. Some had a seat to themselves and at night could lie out in full, rather than slump over in a seat, pushing away the nodding head of the child next to them. Those heads were now nodding off in some stranger's home, in some new bed, and to the sights, sounds, and smells of a new life.

Hellie noticed the change in many of them, especially James Bradley, who now had only one sister to comfort. When Miss Bergeson and Mr. Evans finally came into the car to pass out dinner sandwiches, James rose and yelled, "You said we could all stay together!"

"Now, James, I said it would be perfect *if* you could all stay together. Now what are the chances we can find a family who wants four children?" Miss Bergeson said, with a smile of stony logic.

"No, Mr. Whitaker said we could all stay together! That's what the liar said!"

"James, please," Mr. Evans said, in a calm, low voice. "We are doing the best we can. Eddy and Carla will be just fine together. You know how close they are. Now they can stay together. Those people were very happy to provide them a warm, comfortable, safe home. I would think you would show a little gratitude or at least be happy for them. And once you are all settled, we'll make sure you can write to each other."

"No! Cindy and me are getting off at the next stop and finding our way back. I don't care! If we don't get adopted, then I'll get a job. We're not splitting up!" James said. "Ma never would have wanted it this way!"

His sister, Cindy, was in her seat, crying uncontrollably. "Don't you think you should be tending to Cindy? Don't you think she needs you, James?" Miss Bergeson said. "I promise, you will both feel better about this tomorrow. Perhaps you should pray on this. After dinner, I'll come and pray with you."

James looked back at Cindy. He returned to her and tried to comfort her. "Don't worry, Cindy. I'll figure something out."

Lizzie leaned over her seat and said to Hellie. "Told you."

"Well, I'm with James. He should jump this train and go back to get them."

"He won't," Lizzie whispered. "Miss Bergeson will pray him out of doing that. She's got ways. She'll wear him down with prayer. I've seen it happen over and over again."

Hellie had to admit, when it came to Miss Bergeson, Lizzie knew what she was talking about. Their "guardian" returned later and sat next to James for two hours, and by the time she got up to leave, he was lost in a fervent prayer. Hellie hoped he was praying Bergie would just walk off the end of the train.

Since the moment they met, she and Miss Bergeson had kept a cautious distance. Hellie had worked to keep a civil tongue in her head, but if she remained "seen and not heard" around Bergeson, it was because she was too busy with other matters. Where was she going and what was she going to do once she got there? How long would her money last? What job could she get? Or maybe she should settle in a big town where she could blend in and employ her slick street skills.

Hellie stared at her ghostlike reflection in the window; whatever countryside they were streaming through was nothing but an endless black ocean. She figured anything could be out there . . . cornfields? cows? Indians? whales? The only light was the blurry reflection of the night lights in the orphan car. She had to strain to recognize the sound of the train—by now so constant and nearly a part of her own heartbeat. If it weren't for the gentle movement of the train as it sped along, she could almost imagine she was sitting still.

"Hey, Lizzie," Hellie said, poking her friend. "Wake up."

"Shhhh!" Lizzie said. "Don't you dare wake up Joey. It took me half the night to get him to sleep," she whispered. She tucked Joey's blanket into the train seat, then looked over to Hellie. "What?"

"Where you figure the end of the line's going to be?"

"Can we talk about this tomorrow? I'm sleepy."

"Think we'll get far as Frisco? Sure would like to see that Pacific Ocean out there."

Lizzie sat on an elbow and ran her hand through her hair. Her uneven face and her drooping, lifeless eye were fully exposed and looked even eerier in the faint light of the coach.

"Bergie goes only as far as she has to," Lizzie said. "When all the orphans are taken. That could happen tomorrow. 'Cept me, of course."

"And me," Hellie said.

Lizzie looked at her and asked, "For real, Hellie? For real you're going to run away?"

"Yep."

"You can't be on your own. You're too young."

"Been on my own all my life."

"No, you haven't. Your brother watched over you."

"Ha! I watched over him most times. Anyways, I'm going as far as this train goes. Maybe farther."

"How?"

"I can buy me a ticket, can't I?"

"Yeah, if you had any money."

Hellie wondered if she trusted Lizzie enough to tell her about the false-bottomed valise under her seat. "Well, I got ways of getting money."

"Shhhst!" came a long hiss from the front of the car as Mr. Evans popped his head up from his seat.

"And just what are you going to do for a living, Hellie? Open a charm school?" Lizzie whispered.

"Hey, I could be a professional orphan and sell myself out, then just run off and do it again in the next town," Hellie said. "What a skin game!"

Lizzie tried to stifle her giggling, but couldn't. Hellie tried to shush her, but only seemed to make it worse.

At this, other children stirred and Joey began to whimper. Hellie looked up and saw the black shadow of Mr. Evans standing over her. He pointed to the car in front of them, and Hellie knew she was about to spend another night in the baggage car.

She grabbed her valise and went without saying a word. Don't matter, Hellie thought. She preferred the quiet of the baggage car, where Amanda sometimes came to smoke and talk and show Hellie how the cameras and lens and flashes all worked together to freeze a moment in time.

Five days after getting shot, Harry was discharged from the hospital and given ointment and fresh bandages for his wound and aspirin for his pain. What he really wanted—*really* wanted—was more of that stuff they injected in him to keep the pain of surgery at bay. He'd known about morphine, cocaine, and heroin from the gangs that dealt drugs. He knew about addiction and its downhill slide. But once Harry experienced the euphoric state, the dumb, who-the-hell-cares attitude that morphine delivered, he figured he could handle it. So, before he left, he found the dispensary, broke inside, and started to look for the necessary items.

The black orderly stood with his broom and watched Harry as he rummaged through the drugs, looking for the needles and syringes. When Harry saw him watching, he just stared back at him.

"Don't think you're the first to go looking for Sister Mary," the orderly said.

"I don't know any Sister Mary," Harry said, his arm now swinging painfully outside the sling.

"Oh, you will, you will. Nope, you ain't the first convert and sure as hell you won't be the last."

Harry looked at him and said, "Look, I got money. How about you help me?"

The man shot him a menacing grin and said, "You don't got a dime, son."

Harry pulled his jacket out of his canvas bag and tore through the pockets. He held his jacket up to the orderly and said, "I had twenty-five bucks in here, you son of a bitch!"

"Wasn't me, boy. And you watch who you're calling a son of a bitch!"

"Then who took it?"

"I believe St. Anne took it."

"Who are all these women you keep talking about?"

"Well, this is St. Anne's hospital. And Sister Mary—well, that's just sort of a sweetheart name for God's medicine. You know, morphine. What you're coastin' on right now."

"So, my money went to the hospital?"

"You didn't think all this gracious hospitality was free, did you? Just because it's a charity hospital, don't mean it's all charity. That money went to pay your bills, son."

"It was stole!"

The man laughed and continued his sweeping. "Yep, yep, stole right out from underneath you."

"No one had a right to lift that money!" Harry said, feeling the sharp pain in his shoulder return.

"You telling me your life ain't worth twenty-five dollars?" the man asked, now looking at Harry with a sad smile of mockery.

"Look, alls I want is something for the pain and to get out of here. I'll make it worth your while."

The orderly laughed, "I'm sure you will. I'm leaving the ward now. You just go about your business. I'll see you again soon, though." He poked his head back into the dispensary and added, "See, I clean up the morgue every Tuesday. I'll see you. Sooner or later. Now, if you're smart, you'll put away that dope gun and hype stick. Let ol' Sister Mary have her way with someone else. This ain't the side of Sister Mary you want to be on."

He tipped his white stocking hat, smiled, and left.

Harry was alone in the dispensary. He could feel a small bead of sweat form on his upper lip. The pain was excruciating.

He grabbed the morphine, syringe, and needle and stuffed them into the canvas bag. Then he pulled his coat on over his shoulder, and walked out of the ward and back onto the streets where Flip was pitching pennies out front, ready to join up with him.

The wonder of traveling by train, Hellie thought, was falling asleep in one landscape and waking up to an entirely different one. What a miracle forward motion was. She looked out the window and wondered what state they were in. The rolling hills were not nearly as green here and the trees now looked fuller and more protective of the barns and houses in tight little groves of family.

As the train slowed down, Hellie joined the other orphans to see what sort of town they were approaching this time. It was similar to the dozens of other small towns they had traveled through on Bergeson's carefully plotted route. She saw the platform, the station, and the town beyond, all red brick against the blue sky and the yellowish white of the wheat fields beyond. As red, white, and blue as the Fourth of July.

The train came to a stop. Miss Bergeson clapped her hands to get the children's attention. "Children, some announcements before we proceed. First of all, I want you all to stay away from that photographer woman. Tell her 'no, you can't take my picture.'" She was looking directly at Lizzie and Hellie, who secretly nudged each other.

"Secondly, this town of Cornwall is a very, very special town."

"What state we in?" someone called out.

"We are in Iowa."

"Never heard of it," Hellie said to Lizzie.

"Yes, boys and girls, you will all feel very welcomed here. For you see, Cornwall has recently suffered a tremendous loss."

That caught the attention of the children.

"The Lord saw fit to bring a great tragedy on Cornwall, and they lost several children when a tornado struck a schoolhouse. In all, twelve precious young souls were lost. So, you can see, there will be many, many people here who are missing their own children."

Hellie's face contorted with confusion. She said to Lizzie, "Is she saying what I think she's saying?"

Lizzie nodded and then indicated Miss Bergeson was staring at her.

"Helena, do you have something you wish to share with the rest of us?" she asked.

"Matter of fact, I do," Hellie said.

"Then by all means, stand up and tell us," Miss Bergeson said, running her gold cross back and forth along its chain.

Hellie stood up and said, "Why do you think the Lord would see fit to take away twelve precious little souls just to turn right around and replace 'em with us? I mean, ain't that sort of a lot of work? Working up a tornado, having to listen to all them grieving families, getting this train here. Why you figure He don't just keep things the way they was?"

All orphan faces went back to Miss Bergeson for her response.

Miss Bergeson straightened and seemed to throw her shoulders back like she was preparing for a fistfight. "I can see you are as far behind on your religious schooling as you are on your grammar schooling. Let me just say, Helena, that the Lord works in mysterious ways."

"Aw, He don't work at all," Hellie said, "not if He's sending out them tornadoes and killing twelve children what never did nothing to deserve it."

"Oh, Helena, I am going to pray for your soul," Miss Bergeson said. "Now, we will *all* pray," she continued, staring down at Hellie.

The children dutifully bowed their heads. Hellie looked out the window.

"Lord, please let these precious lambs help to soothe the broken hearts and troubled souls of these people of Cornwall who have already suffered such grievous losses. And Lord, we ask that You let Helena Smith see the wisdom of Your infinite ways."

Hellie tried to figure out which folks on the platform had a broken heart and which folks had a troubled soul.

"We ask it in the name of our Lord, amen," Miss Bergeson finished. Mr. Evans motioned to her that they should proceed. "All right, children, off we go. Two by two."

Hellie and Lizzie were the last. Hellie passed Miss Bergeson, then said, "You don't bother praying for my soul. I think you got all you can handle praying for your own."

"Whatever do you mean?"

"You know what I mean."

Miss Bergeson folded her arms and said, "No, enlighten me."

"Taking advantage of them 'broken hearts' and 'troubled souls,'" Hellie said, nodding toward the people on the platform. "That's plain sinful."

The slap came hard and fast.

After Cornwall, they continued on to Nebraska, where they had a few stops and two layovers and were now minus eleven more orphans. The next stop on Miss Bergeson's tour was Omaha.

"You been in Nebraska before?" said Hellie.

Lizzie said, "No. Bergeson never takes the same route twice."

"Why not?"

Lizzie's face went blank, as though she had never wondered why. "Well, maybe it's because she doesn't want to take a chance of any of the children being returned. You know, if they aren't working out."

"Never return to the scene of the crime," Hellie said.

Lizzie looked out over the town and said, "I wonder sometimes what's become of all those children, in all those homes. If they're happy or maybe already run away. I came close to getting placed out in Missouri. These folks came right up on the stage and worked my arm like a pump handle."

"Real friendly, huh?"

Lizzie cast Hellie a sweet, half-amused, half-sad smile. "No, they were seeing how strong I was."

"Did you haul off and slug 'em?" Hellie asked.

"No," she said, now breaking into full laughter. "I wasn't strong enough!"

Miss Bergeson gave them a sleepy glance over her reading spectacles, and they quieted a bit. "I can tell you what she's thinking right now," Lizzie whispered. "She's thinking how glad she is going to be when someone finally takes me."

"Don't forget Joey."

Lizzie turned to Hellie and said, "Hellie, let's make a pact. Let's you and me decide that we're going to stay together."

Hellie sat back. She didn't sign pacts with anyone. Ever. "I ain't getting adopted. And I thought you wanted to be a nun."

"Aw," Lizzie said, looking out over the golden countryside of Nebraska, "that was just talk. I'm not even Catholic. Besides, I like boys too much to be a nun. I want to get married someday." Her chest heaved with a sigh long held in, and her eye welled with a tremendous tear.

"What?" Hellie asked.

"If I don't find someone to love me while I'm young, you know, looking the way I do, then what's going to happen when I'm old?" She crumpled into the window and hid her face.

"Aw, don't cry," Hellie said. "Come on now, Lizzie. Don't let Bergie see you cry."

Lizzie sat up and sniffed and used the hem of her petticoat to blow her nose. "I mean, look at Bergie. Dried-up old maid. I don't want to end up like her. And she's got all her face! Everyone hates her."

"Yeah, but not because she's a old maid. We hate her cause she's plain old mean. Think about that photographer woman, Miss Collier. She ain't married and she's pretty as you please. Travels and takes her pictures. Got her own dreams, not some man's. You just think about Amanda when you think about growing up."

"Know what, Hellie?" she said.

"What?"

"You're the only friend I ever had since I was little. I did have one girl friend once. Lived across the hall. We were maybe four years old, but I remember," Lizzie said.

Hellie felt that uncomfortable hedge again. "What become of her?"

Lizzie sighed out the last of her tears and simply said, "Oh, she fell out the fifth-story window. About then I had to live with some old aunt."

"Why for? Your ma couldn't take care of you?"

"Probably," Lizzie said, now looking down at Mary, her rag doll. "I remember her coming and going, like Ma kept trying."

Hellie wondered if she was going to tell her about her accident. Finally, Hellie whispered, "Was you born that way, Lizzie?"

Lizzie kept her eye on her doll. "No."

"You don't have to say no more. I was being rude. Don't mind me. You don't have to say no more."

"Aren't you two supposed to be working on your presentation?"

They looked up at Miss Bergeson. "We are," Hellie said. "Lizzie was reciting to me and I was reciting to her."

"Would you like to recite to *me*?" she asked, her long fingers fanned out on her slim hips.

"No, we ain't ready."

"We *aren't* ready," Miss Bergeson corrected.

"Well, if you aren't ready and we ain't ready, then let's give it some more practice, then, okay?" Hellie said.

Miss Bergeson opened the watch pinned to her chest and looked at the time. "We are due to stop in Omaha in one hour. These folks are expecting each of you to recite."

"How come we didn't recite nothing back at them other places?"

"Our schedule didn't allow for it. But there will be a nice long afternoon with the folks in Omaha, so you better be ready."

"How can I recite if I can't read?" Hellie asked. Lizzie had already pulled out her Bible and was reading the verse she had picked out.

"A poem or a song will do nicely. Or a favorite prayer. Even the smaller children can sing or recite a nursery rhyme. So, I suggest you work on that rather than chitchat, ladies." She went to the front of the car.

Hellie looked at Lizzie. "For real? You can read all them words?"

"Yes," she said, almost apologetically.

"I know the ABCs, but not how they all make words. Harry could read a little. Didn't do him much good."

"Well, you have to learn how to read, Hellie. Maybe I can teach you."

"I tried a few times. Words just hop all over the page."

"Maybe you need glasses."

"Don't need to know how to read to . . . do what I know how to do," Hellie said.

"I said work on your recitations!" Miss Bergeson shouted over the seats.

Lizzie put her nose into her Bible, and Hellie just looked out over the countryside as the pinks and golds of the early morning claimed the hills.

Harry and Flip had agreed to meet that night after his discharge at Jigger's, a tavern haunt of Harry's. Harry got two blocks before he started to feel faint. His shoulder was burning, and he could actually see his heartbeat through a pulsing in his eyes. He sat on a stoop and rested. He had no money for a trolley or cab, and he didn't think he even had the energy to hitch a ride.

He managed the rest of the distance and slipped into Jigger's. The sudden dark coolness brought back the throbbing dark patches to his eyes, and he fell, almost faint, into a booth.

"You've seen better days," Jigger said, looking down at Harry.

Harry looked up and tried to smile. "Yeah. Flip been around?"

"Not today. Want a beer?"

"Broke, Jigger."

"On the house. You look like a beer would do you good."

Jigger returned with two beers and placed them on the table. Harry inhaled the first one, amazed at the speed in which it hit and numbed his brain. "Thanks. Tastes good."

"So, it's true what I heard," Jigger said.

"What'd you hear?"

"Heard you got shot up. Heard some kid went down blazing," Jigger continued. He sat down in the booth and looked at Harry, gray and disheveled and shaking.

"Just another fun day at the zoo," Harry said.

Jigger shoved the second beer toward him. "How old are you?"

Harry looked at him and said, "If a sermon comes with the beer, I'll pass." He moved the beer toward Jigger.

"Flip said at least you got Hellie out," Jigger continued. "Heading west to find a home, huh?"

Harry stared at Jigger. He hadn't even thought of Hellie in several days. "Look, this shoulder is killing me. They pulled the bullet out and left me sort of mangled." He reached for the needle kit in his pocket and placed it on the table. "They sent me home with this."

Jigger looked at it.

"For the pain," Harry was quick to add. "It's for the pain." Jigger looked at him doubtfully. "Stupid thing is, well, they didn't show me, you know, just how it works. Thought maybe Ruby might know."

"Oh, she'd know all right," Jigger said. "That chronic's been on the needle for years."

"Yeah, I knew that, so maybe you could call Ruby down and she can show me how this all works," Harry said.

Jigger stood up and said, "You know her room number. You go ask her. I'm not going to be a part of that, Harry. And you don't go shooting up in my joint, either, you hear?"

"Sure, Jigger, sure. But it's not shooting up. It's just for the pain."

"Might be for the pain now, boy, but it's going to be for the pleasure real soon."

Harry looked down at the syringe, needle, and vials. Jigger added, "Why don't you just give me all that and I'll put it away? Here, drink your beer and see if that doesn't help."

Harry's eyes were tearing. "This stuff works *real* good," he whispered.

"Look, you're broke, you say? I'll bet Ruby could get fifty bucks for that junk. Maybe more. Couldn't you use that money?"

"Yes," Harry said. "Yes."

"Give it to me." Jigger put his hand out. "Drink your beer. I'll make you a sandwich and you'll feel better. Say, you got some aspirin there. The soldiers in France all swear by it. Takes all the pain away. Take some of those, son. You can sack out in the back room. I'll tell Flip you're here when he comes in."

Slowly, Harry pushed the morphine away. Jigger took it and said, "I'll get Ruby. You'll be all set."

Jigger made good on all of it. The beer, the sandwich, the back room, Ruby's help.

When Harry woke up several hours later, he felt stronger and sturdier than he had since before the shootout. When he inhaled, he didn't have that taste of chemicals that had been with him since the operation. His shoulder barely stung; his head was clear, his vision unblurred.

Flip was sitting across the room, eating a sandwich. On a table between them was a pile of money.

"Hey," Flip said.

"Hey," Harry answered, sitting up.

"We're plush," Flip said, pointing to the money. "Ruby told me to tell you she got over a hundred bucks for, what'd she call it, the whole joker."

Harry fanned the money on the table. "No kidding," he said. "All that for just that little bit of . . ."

"What was it, Harry?"

"Morphine. All that for just a little bit of morphine."

Amanda Beulah Emmaline Collier had all her photography equipment set up and got a shot of the marching orphans just as they were being marshaled into Omaha City Park. Bergeson had arranged for a picnic, complete with the Elks Volunteer Brass Band. Red, white, and blue banners decorated the freshly painted bandstand, making it look like a giant patriotic layer cake.

Hellie and Lizzie took up the rear of the orphan procession. Joey was propped on Lizzie's hip, pacifier in his mouth, long dress hiding his deformity, wide-eyed, terrified, looking as though he might burst into hysterics at any moment.

"They celebrate Independence Day early here in Nebraska?" Hellie asked Lizzie.

"No, just one of Bergie's extravaganzas. My first time out, we were all marched right up the middle of town with some old soldiers from the Civil War. I was scared to death I was going to go home with some old coot."

They passed Amanda, who was looking into one of her camera lenses. "Ladies!" she called out.

The girls stopped and looked into the camera lens.

"Now children, stay together. Elizabeth and Helena! You may *not* pose for that photographer-woman! You just come right up here next to me." Then, to Amanda, she said, "I will tell the sheriff, who I know personally, that you are bothering the children and for you to cease and desist."

"When the children complain, I will cease and desist. This is a public place and I have every right to photograph anything, or anyone, I wish."

Hellie was watching with interest as the two women squared off. Her money was on Amanda, but she was armed with a heavy camera. Using just fists, Hellie thought the wiry Bergie could take her.

Miss Bergeson whirled away and gathered the children toward the picnic area, where she was greeted by city matrons in an array of creamy beige, sky blue, and stately gray dresses and swooping matching summer hats.

Picnic tables were adorned with red and white checkered cloths, and on each were several fliers, anchored with glasses of lemonade. Hellie picked one up as they marched to their own tables in front of the bandstand. There were the name tags on the tables where each child was supposed to sit, don the tag, and remain, smiling politely as good orphans should.

"Ever been to a horse race?" Hellie asked Lizzie.

"No."

"Before each race, all the folks come and look at the horses to see which ones to bet on." She handed the paper to Lizzie. "Here. What's this? The racing form?"

Lizzie, having seen dozens of similar fliers, simply glanced at it and said, "Says stuff about us and our bad lives so folks will want to save us."

"Yep. It's a racing form. What's it say about me?"

"Says you were found begging for food off of Broadway in New York City and you like sewing and . . ."

"That's a dang lie! Everyone knows Broadway ain't good for panhandling. Guess I did sew a button on once."

"It's just advertising, Hellie. They have to tell these people something."

"What's it say about you?"

At this Lizzie held the flier in front of her and said officiously, "Miss Elizabeth Coultrane, known as Lizzie, fourteen years old. Former Queen of Queens and Empress of the Holy Washtub." Then, to Hellie,

"That's like a Holy Grail, only bigger. Miss Coultrane seeks a rich family with maids and black servants and white horses wearing pure silver saddles. Miss Coultrane's unique appearance comes from years of work upon the stage."

"It doesn't say that," Hellie said, taking the flier and folding it into an airplane. Just as she was taking aim at a tall, feathered hat, the plane disappeared out of her grasp and Miss Bergeson ripped it in half.

A lunch was served. The band played something patriotic. Speeches were made, and finally Miss Bergeson announced the children would now be available to chat with those who were interested. As before, she advised that questions about their pasts should politely be avoided.

Hellie toed the line. She curtsied as instructed, said please and thank you and sir and ma'am. Lizzie held up to the inevitable, sympathetic "oh mys" and startled "oh dears," and with each frown, gasp, and quick turn to a handy distraction, Hellie saw Lizzie had more grit than she had given her credit for.

One couple, middle-aged and well dressed, kept coming back to Hellie with more questions and the third time with their own little girl.

The woman said, smiling sweetly, "We wanted you two to get acquainted. My gosh, you two girls even look a little alike. Now Darla, Daddy and I will be right over there, talking to Miss Bergeson."

"I'm adopted, too," little Darla announced. "Came here on a train, just like you."

Hellie looked down at the child's face, so clean and polished it seemed to shine. "That's nice."

"We have a new Model T."

"Well lah-de-dah."

"Momma says I need a sister on account of I miss my real sister. She's someplace in India-nana, so I'm lonely. Do you like dolls?"

"Look, I'm not good sister material," Hellie said. "Go peddle your papers to little Susan over there. She's only four. You can teach her how to be a good sister."

"Can't you be my sister?"

"No. Now beat it!" Hellie smiled when she said it, knowing eyes were upon her. Darla was probably as nice a little girl as one could ever meet. Probably, if one *had* to have a family, if one *had* to have a sister, Darla was good sister material. But not for Hellie.

Still, Darla and her family persisted, even after Hellie said her mother had been a Jamaican voodoo queen who would reach out from beyond the grave to curse any family who adopted her. If Hellie didn't play her cards right, she could see herself bumping out of town crammed into that new Model T's backseat with little Darla and her dolls for company. Forever. She knew every rat has an escape hole. No self-respecting street arab goes into any situation without a plan. Hellie's plan entailed a street song from back home.

The children were gathered back to their tables, and Miss Bergeson announced each child would now recite for the audience of prospective parents and public officials.

They spouted nursery rhymes and Bible verses. Two children sang a song, and James told a joke. The audience clapped and laughed appropriately, and Hellie could tell Bergie was pretty proud of her little orphan sideshow.

At last, Hellie was called up to the bandstand to perform. Miss Bergeson and Mr. Evans each glared at her as she passed. Hellie smiled sweetly at Darla and her parents, who had come closer to the bandstand.

"And what are you going to recite for us today?" the announcer asked, reading her name tag, "Helena."

"'My Bonnie Lies Over the Ocean,'" she announced. "Only a way we used to sing back home."

Both Mr. Evans and Miss Bergeson's faces turned to stone, and each took a step closer. Then, with a face full of drama, Hellie sang out:

My brudder's a glassy-eyed junkhound,
My sister's a gun-totin' moll,
My kin may be hopheads and mobsters,
But I am da woist of dem all!
Drink up, drink up,
Oh drink up till we're on da floor—or-or
Drink up, drink up
And den we'll drink up some more.
My mudder lies . . .

Mr. Evans snatched Hellie offstage with the expertise of a football linebacker. Amanda captured the silent, stunned faces of the crowd, barely able to hold the camera steady while trying to contain her own laughter.

And Little Darla had a new sister. Susan.

"Where we going?" Flip asked Harry.

"Back to the lysol dump," Harry said, hailing a taxi.

"Da hospital? Why? Thought you was better. Been two weeks."

"I'm fine. I got other business with St. Anne," Harry said, climbing into the backseat of the taxi. "Come on. My treat," he added when Flip hesitated.

"Good hotel and taxies," Flip said. "I knew we was in da dimes, but maybe we ought to cut back some, you know, Harry? I don't know 'bout you, but I ain't joining no army and going to no war just for da cots and hots like some of da boys been doing. I don't care what dey say about dem Frenchie women."

"A peewee like you? Hellie'd stand a better chance of getting in the army than you. You and me got better things to do with our lifes than fighting Germans. Now get in, the meter's running."

The cabbie pulled up in front of St. Anne's Charity Hospital. "You wait here, okay, Flip?" Harry said. "And stay low. You never know when C. K. and his sidewalk committee will show their mugs."

"Saw Willie yesterday! Did I tell you? Him and some other boys was working da boardwalk down at Coney," Flip said.

"C. K. anywheres around?" Harry asked.

"Didn't see him, but you got to figure he was close by."

"They didn't see you, did they?"

"Nah, I was under da boardwalk, looking for coins and cigarette butts."

Harry gave him a playful shove and said, "Looking up women's skirts, you little peeper. I'll be back."

Harry vanished into the hospital, and Flip found a shady tree to hide behind.

"Pssst! Hey, you!" Harry called in a loud whisper, hoping to get the black orderly's attention and not that of the nurse at the ward desk. The man looked over the tray he was carrying and came over to Harry in the hallway.

"Man, that dope didn't last you very long. You must got it bad, son."

Harry just pulled up his sleeves and showed him his clean veins. "Followed your advice. This ain't the side of Sister Mary I want to be on."

The orderly put down the tray and said, "Keep talking."

Harry looked down the hall and waited for some people to enter a room before he replied. "They pay you good here? Toting bedpans and mopping up piss and blood?"

"I get by."

"Getting by ain't getting ahead," Harry said with a charming smile.

"Keep talking."

"Look, I got some connections and thought maybe you and me . . . we could enter into a little—well, business arrangement."

"Keep talking." His deep voice was almost without inflection.

"I can find a good home for ol' Sister Mary. You know what I mean?"

"Yeah, I know what you mean, and you think I'm the Pope."

Harry wasn't sure he knew what he meant, but he laughed as though he did. "Yeah, the Pope. Say, what's your name, anyway?"

"Pope."

"No name?"

"Not if we're going into business together."

The rest was easy. They struck a deal whereby the Pope would smuggle morphine out of the dispensary. Adding a measure of sugar to the pot, the Pope said he had a cousin who worked as an orderly uptown where they were sending a lot of the war wounded.

"And those boys come home already addicted," the Pope added. "So what swings in, swings out."

"You mean, those soldiers from Europe? Deal to them? Isn't that . . ."

"Are you a businessman or not?" the Pope asked, ushering Harry into a quiet corner.

"Why sure."

"Look, it won't matter to them one bit where they get their fix. Pretty soon Uncle Sam will cut them off and that's where we step in. You know, I knew all along you were one smart kid. I've been waiting for a slick white article like you to come along for some time now. You see, there's only so much us black folk can sell on the streets."

"Well, good, then. Good," Harry said. They shook hands, agreed on a percentage breakdown, and arranged their first drop.

The Pope walked Harry out of the ward and showed him the stairs. "Best you stay clear of this place from now on, Harry. You let the Pope do his part. Every day, I'll call you and tell you what we have so's you'll know how much cash to bring. We drop the next day."

"They'll know where to find me at this number," Harry said, writing a phone number on a piece of paper. "It's just a beanery, but I'm always there."

Harry couldn't shake an odd feeling as he took the fire escape stairs down to the lobby. He hadn't expected getting into the drug racket to be so easy, but then, he hadn't expected Ruby to sell the load at such a high price. Maybe it was the war—everything else was being rationed. Stood to reason morphine was in pretty high demand these days.

Flip saw him exit the hospital and came up to him. "Dat didn't take long," he said, putting his cap back on.

Harry looked back at the third floor and said, "No, it didn't, did it?"

"Where we heading now, Harry? You gonna show me more pickpocketing tricks? You promised."

"Nope, Flip. Those days are over. Come on. We're heading above the line. Nothing but swell joints uptown from now on."

One by one, sometimes two by two, the orphans disappeared—some quietly and with amazing dignity, others screaming and with clinging tears—into the homes of strangers dotted across the route Bergeson had so carefully plotted out. After the Omaha song incident, Miss Bergeson stuck so close to Hellie during orphan stops that Hellie thought they may as well have been shackled together like chain-gangers. During interviews, she was allowed to state only her name and her age and even that only when asked.

Amanda had a difficult time getting posed photographs and proceeded to get candid ones instead. Lizzie was told she could not converse with Hellie, but was ordered to read the Bible to Hellie during the long, hot hours riding the train.

So it was Genesis through Leviticus along the North Platte River in Nebraska, Numbers through Judges as they creased the corner of Wyoming, and by the time they steamed into Pocatello, Idaho, Lizzie had gotten through Samuel 1 and 2.

In Pocatello just three orphans returned from that morning's placing out and climbed wearily aboard the train—Lizzie, Joey, and Hellie—Lizzie for her face, Joey for his clubfoot, and Hellie for her inevitable lack of charm toward anyone who showed even a remote interest in her.

Hellie commandeered the right side of the orphan car, and Lizzie took over the left side. Miss Bergeson had sent Mr. Evans back to New

York, and she now sat in the front of the car and simply smiled at her three charges, as though holding in a wicked secret. She fanned herself with the telegram she'd received in Pocatello. When she finally nodded off, Hellie and Lizzie jumped the seats to join each other and talk.

"Reckon we're in Timbuktu by now," Hellie said. It was hot, and they had opened several windows. Hellie took in a deep breath and, with it, foreign smells. "Hmm, smells sort of sweet. Where do you reckon we are now, Lizzie?"

"I don't know. Guess maybe Oregon by now."

"Dang, that Pacific Ocean's gotten be coming up soon."

Lizzie looked up from her doll, Mary, recalling her geography. "Idaho, then Oregon, then the Pacific Ocean. Even I've never been this far before. Furthest I got was my first trip out. Got to Denver. Gee, I thought that was the end of the earth."

Several hours later, Miss Bergeson left wearing dusty black travel togs, but returned wearing a summery yellow dress with white accents. Both Hellie and Lizzie looked up, stunned. She was far from beautiful, but she was also far from the widowy Bergeson they had both grown accustomed to seeing.

"Well, ladies," she said, adjusting her cross so it peeked shyly through her modest cleavage, "we are coming into Pendleton."

"Or-i-gon?" Hellie asked.

"Yes, Oregon." Then she added with her acidic smile, "This is the last stop on our journey."

"Too bad you ain't got more merchandise," Hellie said, indicating the now-empty orphan car.

"I think we'll all do just fine," she said. The train jerked to a stop. There wasn't the usual fanfare of local dignitaries waiting outside. No banners, no bands, no indication at all that an orphan train had arrived.

"Come with me," Bergeson said. "Bring your things." She leaned down to pick up Joey who was just finishing his bottle.

Hellie and Lizzie looked at each other. "Bring our every things?" Hellie asked.

"Yes, bring your belongings. I have found all of you a home."

Lizzie's face froze. "Sight unseen?" she asked.

"It took some fancy phone calls and pulling a few strings, but this is where I finally wash my hands of you all. Oh, this is a fine placement. Some of my best work, really. You both will be together and you both will be sisters."

Neither girl moved.

Miss Bergeson turned back around and demanded, "That *is* what you want, isn't it? This woman has wanted two girls for some time now. Everyone wins."

Hellie felt her heart race. She wanted west. Well, she was west. She wanted the end of the line. Well, this was the end of the line. Now what?

"Meet me on the platform in ten minutes. That's just enough time to clean up a bit." She grabbed Joey's travel bag and took him to the convenience car to change him.

"What do we do?" Lizzie asked.

"We go along with it. Get the lay."

"What's that?"

"You know, see what's what. See what our opportunities are. We come all this way, after all."

"I'm scared, Hellsbells."

"What's to be scared of? It's them that ought to be scared." She indicated the town outside the window. Lizzie hesitated. Hellie said, "Hey, this might be a sweet deal. No telling what's waiting out there. Come on. Bergie's waiting."

She led Lizzie into the ladies' room in the car ahead of them. Hellie washed her face, positioned her hair bow, dusted off her travel skirt, and ran tooth powder over her teeth with her finger. She helped Lizzie comb her long hair so it hid much of the damaged side of her face. They stood, looking at each other in the smoky reflection of the mirror.

Hellie smiled, but her mind was racing almost as fast as her heart. Middle of nowhere in a Timbuktu state called Oregon—a state she hadn't even known existed. Just a few weeks ago she was pitching pennies, picking pockets, swilling stolen beer, and shooting wharf rats with her slingshot. A few weeks ago, she had a brother, she had street prospects, and she was free as air.

A few weeks ago, her brother was planning on ditching her the way she was now planning on ditching Lizzie.

A.B.E. Collier, for the first time, was nowhere to be seen, either on the train platform or the large, red-brick station beyond. The heat of the late June day seemed to radiate from the bricks, and there was a brittle dryness to the air that Hellie had never felt before. That, along with Lizzie's hesitant, timid glances around, made Hellie all the more uneasy.

"Guess this is the West," Lizzie said, noticing some horses tied to a fence post placed between two parked Model T's. Two men, dressed in jeans and cowboy boots, came out of the building and donned large cowboy hats as they did. "Just like cowboys in the moving pictures," she added.

"Quick, girls!" Amanda said as she rounded the corner of the train depot.

"What?" Hellie asked. "Where's Bergie?"

"She's inside talking to your . . . new . . . well, guardian. I want one last photograph of you two." She ushered the girls to a patch of sunlight.

"What's she like?" Lizzie asked.

"You'll find out soon enough. Smile, won't you, Lizzie?"

"I am smiling," she replied, looking tentatively around.

Hellie and Lizzie stood next to each other while Amanda continued. "I want to thank you girls for all your help. You've made my job much easier. Hold it."

Flash!

"One more."

Hellie didn't smile for either photo. She felt that now-familiar knot tighten in her stomach, and try as she might, could not explain it or demand it lessen its grip. Lizzie sat on some luggage and hid her doll.

"Where are you going?" Hellie asked Amanda as she was hurrying to put away her camera.

"I'm getting back on that train to Portland, then heading down to San Francisco."

"Always wanted to see Frisco," Hellie said.

"Then, I'm going to insist Mr. Hearst buy my story," Amanda continued.

"But, you was going to show me more about how your camera works. And the flashy thing," Hellie said, her words falling away. "Say, maybe I could go with you and . . ."

But Amanda wasn't listening. She was busy pinning her hair back and organizing her luggage. She approached Hellie as though to hug her, but Hellie stepped back and said, "Nice knowing you." She offered her hand.

Amanda shook her hand and said to Lizzie. "Now, don't you girls worry. They say she's the richest woman around. Hellie, save your money and you can buy a Brownie camera at any drugstore." She looked around. "I'll bet even in a cow town like this."

The whistle blew, and Amanda scooted off and vanished around the corner just as Miss Bergeson and two women came out of the train depot. One woman was well dressed in elegant light grays. She was short and very thin and, even with the use of a cane, walked with a nose-forward attitude. The other woman, following behind and carrying little Joey, was stout and sturdy. A long gray braid wound off her shoulder like a snake, and Joey was tasting its wispy tail.

"There you are, girls," Miss Bergeson cooed.

Lizzie slowly reached for Hellie's hand, gripped it tight, and whispered, "Richest woman around."

"I want you to meet Mrs. Gorence. She wants two girls to add to her family. This is Helena Smith and this is Elizabeth Coultrane. Lizzie is fourteen and we think Helena is thirteen. As I mentioned, we have no record of her birth," Miss Bergeson went on, showing Mrs. Gorence her papers.

Mrs. Gorence stepped forward to get a closer look. "What happened to your face?" she bluntly asked Lizzie, pushing back the locks of hair.

Lizzie looked at Miss Bergeson.

"She's asking you, not me," Miss Bergeson said. "You may tell her."

Lizzie looked down and said, "Accident. Scars'll go away. Eye won't grow back, though."

"No, I guess eyes don't grow back, do they?" Mrs. Gorence said back to Miss Bergeson. "First it's a lame baby and now a half-blind girl. And what about you?" she asked Hellie. "How damaged are you?"

Hellie looked her in the eye, noting she was about her own height, maybe just over five feet. If she had two bits for every time she'd squared off with a street punk this size, she'd be rich. But this was no street punk.

"Well, I don't need no cane," she said, with a cagey glance toward the woman's feet.

Miss Bergeson was quick to say, "I have found Helena's only shortcoming is her sassy tongue and her lack of schooling. She knows her alphabet, but she can't read."

"Does this one read?"

"Oh yes. Lizzie is quite a good reader. She can do sums, too."

"I'm not totally convinced about this one," she said, inspecting Hellie as she circled her. "A bit of a runt, and I'll bet she has her adult height. Have you started your monthlies?"

Hellie now walked around the woman in the same way and said, "Where do you think that little baby come from?"

Miss Bergeson grabbed Hellie by the arm and whisked her around the corner. When they came back, Hellie smiled and said, "I'm sorry I said that, ma'am. It was just a joke. Little Joey ain't my baby at all. I was just pulling your—I was just funning. No, I ain't—haven't—started all that monthly business yet and I think I'll grow some. I'm strong for my size."

"And I'm not sure I like that look in her eyes. How long has she lived on the streets?"

"Oh, not long," Miss Bergeson said. "Have you, dear?"

"Just long enough to want a real home," Hellie said, recalling another orphan's line. She gave the old woman her widest smile.

The conductor shouted, "All aboard for Portland!" Hellie watched Amanda board the train, and she wished like hell she could run out of this mess and jump that train.

"Well, then, it's all settled," Miss Bergeson said. "So, shall we sign those papers? Here, you can use my back." She handed the woman a pen and the papers and offered her long, flat back.

The girls were told to wait in the back of a buckboard wagon loaded with supplies and drawn by two black horses. The woman holding Joey waited with them.

Lizzie grabbed Hellie and said, "What did Bergie say to you?"

"Said I was going to ruin it for you and Joey if I spouted off any more. Said we was an all-or-nothing deal with that old lady."

"Oh," Lizzie said.

Hellie jumped up and said, "Uh oh. I got to find the necessary."

The woman holding Joey said, "In the depot. Best hurry."

Hellie jumped down from the buckboard, snagging her skirt on the tailgate hatch. She whirled and snatched it back with a snap, tearing it so the hem dragged. She scrambled up onto the train platform.

It was a fast escape—too fast, not planned out, the kind of escape Harry would have hollered on her for making, she thought as she watched the train pull out. Now what? Everything she needed to strike out on her own was in her valise in that wagon with Lizzie. Didn't matter. She could hit town, roll a drunk, pick a pocket or two, get on the train back to . . . where? Anywhere she damn well wanted. But where was that?

She moved forward, but was jerked back as though her skirts were stuck again. "Going somewhere?"

She whirled around to face Mrs. Gorence. She could smell the powder on her cheeks, see the fine lines around her lips. Her eyes were brown and haloed with gray.

"You got Lizzie and you got Joey. You don't need me."

"I need *two* girls and had to take the cripple baby to get them. Now get back in that wagon or I'll . . ."

"What?" Hellie challenged. "You'll what?"

"*Put* you in it," the woman said, matching the challenge in Hellie's voice.

"You and what army?"

"That army," she said, indicating a large, tall man now standing behind Hellie.

Hellie turned around. She looked up at the man. A kind face. No henchman, she figured, but strong enough to carry her under one arm, Lizzie under the other, and probably balance little Joey on his head. She looked down at the wagon and saw Lizzie waving for her to come back down.

Hellie said, "You win this one."

"You win this one . . . what?" Mrs. Gorence led.

"You win this one . . . madam."

"'Ma'am' will do."

Hellie looked down at Mrs. Gorence's cane, anchoring the ripped hem of her skirt. The woman stepped aside and Hellie turned to follow the man, the Gorence army, down the step and to the wagon below, while Mrs. Gorence limped away toward town.

Hellie, Lizzie, the gray-braided woman, and Joey rode in the back of the
wagon, sitting among large sacks of flour and sugar, crates, and two
huge saddles. The man drove the wagon and handled the two gigantic
draft horses like they were gentle little ponies.

Hellie tried not to stare at the woman who was looking curiously
now into the sweet, dozing face of Joey. She was dark and high-cheeked,
and Hellie wondered if maybe she was an Indian woman like she'd seen
in some Wild West pictures. The woman flicked away a bothersome
fly and then unfolded the light blanket around his legs. She inspected
his clubfoot, picked it up, moved it this way and that, bent his knee,
and when he showed signs of waking, simply tucked it back out of the
burning sun and rocked him with a gentle, "Shhh, shhh."

"Where we heading?" Hellie finally asked the woman.

She pointed toward the dirt road ahead in the morning sun and said,
"Exactly five hundred and sixteen electricity poles ahead to the Hills.
Home."

Both Lizzie and Hellie followed her point. A gust of hot wind blew
Lizzie's long hair away from her face. The woman looked at her with
the same curious inspection she had used when she'd looked at Joey's
clubfoot.

"I have some salve for your face," she said, a small smile coming to
her full, dark lips.

Lizzie grabbed her hair and brought it back around to cover her face.

Sensing her embarrassment, Hellie asked, looking around them, "So what sort of place is these hills?"

"Big," the woman answered, smiling now at her.

At that, the driver leaned back and added, "Some say *too* big."

"That ol' lady. She holding heavy? You know, rich?" Hellie asked.

Lizzie slapped her leg and said, "Hellie, that's rude. She means, will we each have our own room?"

The woman looked at her, then shrugged.

"She sure must like children," Lizzie said, "to take us all on like this. Even a cripple."

The woman looked across the wagon to the girls and her knowing smile got even bigger. The driver looked down at the woman. "You going to tell 'em, Birdy?" he asked. "Or wait and let 'em see for themselves?"

"Here's a hint," the woman, Birdy, said. "How much do you like cows?" She indicated the horizon dotted with grazing cattle.

"I like 'em fine, long as they're on a platter with catsup," Hellie replied sarcastically, trying to define a new smell in the dry wind . . . manure? Dead animals? Cesspool?

"On a platter with catsup!" the driver echoed, laughing. "I never met a cow I didn't prefer that way!"

They passed under a large wrought-iron gateway.

"What's that say?" Hellie asked Lizzie, pointing to the large letters scrolled into the ironworks.

"The Hidden Hills," Lizzie said.

Then, from the road behind, a puff of dust billowed after an approaching automobile. Then several horn honks, followed by the wagon driver pulling the team over so the car could pass. In the car, top down, drove Mrs. Gorence. She did not so much as wave or look their way. She just passed and continued, leaving them to fend off the thick dust from the road.

They continued for another half hour, the sun now higher in the sky and the heat beginning to beat down. Birdy had put up a large umbrella that shaded her and little Joey. They went down a hill and around a bend, and there they were, the Hidden Hills, holding in a valley so green, so unexpected, that Lizzie's face exploded in a huge grin.

"It's beautiful!" she said. "And it really is hidden!" Willows and gray aspens grew along a stream, looking like a fabled oasis. There was a large white house, three stories, surrounded by organized rows of poplars, as though embracing it, keeping it safe and secure. There were several barns, corrals, outbuildings, machines for god knows what, and animals. Horses looked up from their grazing as the wagon lumbered past. The draft horses nickered a hello to pasture mates. Black-and-white cows dotted a hillside, and off in the distance, a sea of blood-red and white cattle seemed to move as one.

"Oh, Hellie, we are rich," Lizzie whispered.

The wagon went up to the house and stopped next to the automobile, which, despite the dust, glistened hot black in the sun. But there was no one there to greet them. The driver got down, and Birdy handed Joey, now awake and wide-eyed, to him. Then she climbed down off the wagon, took the baby, and went up the steps.

Hellie and Lizzie started to get up, but the driver said, "Stay put."

He climbed back aboard and clucked the team to life. The girls looked at the huge house. The windows were all open, white curtains being teased outside by a warm breeze. There were verandahs on both the second and third stories, making it look more like the decks of a land-bound ocean liner. Hellie counted seven chimneys made of rock, sprouting from the roof.

They rumbled past the house, past the garages, past the stables, bunkhouses, migrants' cottages, and two large barns, stuffed to the brim with bales of hay. The road circled up around the back, past a pond, then came to a stop behind the great house. There were three old but well-kept and immaculately whitewashed buildings.

The driver pointed as he announced: "Icehouse, smokehouse, washhouse. I suggest you settle in the washhouse. The other's too cold, that one's too smoky."

Hellie looked at the great house, shaded, but just as imposing from behind as from the front. The white fences, pond, gardens, and lawns were all impeccably kept.

"Who all lives there?" Hellie asked, pointing to the house.

The driver, now pulling down their belongings and piling them on the porch of the washhouse, simply grunted, "Mrs. G., Arla the cook. Now that little cripple baby, I guess. Birdy's got a room off the kitchens."

"And we have to live *here?*" Hellie said, pointing to the washhouse.

"Mrs. G's orders," he said. "Don't worry, you got all the hot water you need. We got lights, too." He pointed to the wires connecting all the buildings. "Ain't so bad in there. We just got us three modern, brand-spanking new washing machines. Ain't like we're sending you down to the river to do the wash on the rocks. You're lucky. Last girls lasted two or three months. And I cleaned out the snakes and spiders just last week." He laughed when he saw their stricken faces. "I'm joking, girls." He climbed aboard the wagon and added, "I cleaned 'em all out just yesterday. Birdy'll be around to get you settled," he said. "You need anything, just come looking for me. My name is Perry. I'm foreman, handyman, and official hirer and firer. I'm always handy."

Alone on the porch to the washhouse, Lizzie and Hellie looked at each other. Together, they pushed the door open. Lizzie fumbled for the light switch and turned it on.

They were welcomed with the smell of bleach and soap and a cushioned blast of moist heat. The large room had two elevated hot-water tanks that serviced the three wood-and-metal washing machines hooked to a long sink with snakelike rubber hoses.

Hellie inspected a machine and said, "Wonder how you crank them wringers."

"I think they crank themselves," said Lizzie. "Look. They're electric." She pointed to the wires that wound up and into the open-beamed ceiling where they intertwined with an intricate colony of cobwebs. "Remind me to cut my hair," Lizzie added.

"What for?"

"I've heard about girls' hair and hands and . . ."

Their eyes met and each other knew what other matronly parts could get stuck in a laundry wringer. They giggled, but nervously.

The side door led to the backyard, all nicely clipped grass under the rows and rows of laundry lines, each anchored on the ends by white-painted crosses. Several sheets were hanging, crisp and stiffened by the sun. Their bright whiteness almost hurt Hellie's eyes.

"Look," Lizzie said, peeping into the back room. They went in and found four beds, built-ins along the walls, drawers underneath. Neat, crisp, organized. A table and four chairs in the center, a well-stocked bookshelf, a woodburning stove in the corner, and old rag rug on the floor.

"Guess maybe we ain't so rich after all," Lizzie said, a frown of disappointment covering half her face.

Hellie took one look their future, grabbed Lizzie, tromped along the manicured gravel pathways, around to the main house, up the grand steps,
through the twin glass-beveled doors, inspecting each room until she
found Mrs. Gorence sitting in a small parlor.

"I think there's been a mistake," Hellie announced to Mrs. Gorence.

"I beg your pardon," the woman said, her cup of coffee halfway to
her mouth. "Who let you in?"

"*I* let me in!"

"Well, let yourself out," she said, indicating the back of the house.
"The help is always to use the back entrance."

Hellie just crossed her arms in front of her like she had seen Harry
do countless times when he was challenging a rival gang. "Lizzie and
me think there's been a mistake."

Mrs. Gorence looked around the room. "Lizzie?"

Hellie looked around and found that rather than standing toe to toe
with Hellie, Lizzie had stayed behind in the hall, her feet barely visible
around the corner. Hellie pulled her into the room.

"This is Lizzie," Hellie said. "I'm Hellie and this is Lizzie."

Mrs. Gorence put down her cup, put on her reading glasses, and inspected the folded legal papers on the table in front of her. "Says here
Elizabeth and Helena."

"It could say Goldilocks and Snow White," Hellie said, "but this is
Lizzie and I am Hellie. Now, are them the papers what makes us yours?"

She put the papers down and said, a slight lilt of mockery in her voice, "Them's the papers."

"Well, there's been a mistake. We ain't no Chinee laundry workers. Your man took us out back to some washhouse, but them papers says we're getting a new home, not a new job."

"Hellie, I don't think . . . ," Lizzie said in a small voice.

"Speak up, girl!" Mrs. Gorence said. "You're half-blind, not half-witted. At least that's what the papers say."

"Um, I was just saying maybe we should . . ."

"No, we shouldn't!" Hellie broke in. "We're orphans, not hired hands. You want to adopt us, well, we can stay on like, well, on approval, but putting us to work in a laundry ain't part of the deal."

Mrs. Gorence again referred to the papers. She pointed to the large writing at the top and said, "And what does it say right here?"

That set Hellie back. "Go ahead, Lizzie, read it."

Lizzie took a timid step closer. She turned her head sideways so her good eye could read.

"In-den-ture of female child. This in-den-ture, dated this nineteenth day of June . . ."

"You can stop," Mrs. Gorence said, taking the papers away. "It says indenture, not adoption."

"What's indenture?" Hellie asked.

Birdy had entered the room with a silver coffee pot, and she added coffee to Mrs. Gorence's cup. She stood in attendance behind the sofa.

"In short, it's an agreement between myself and the Society for Friendless Children in New York. I agree to certain terms for the next three years in exchange for three years of work from you girls."

"Ain't that slavery?" Hellie demanded.

"No, it's business."

"Come on, Lizzie."

"Now stop and think, my dears. Where would you be—*what* would you be, if you weren't here?"

"Free," Hellie retorted.

"Hardly. You are legally in my charge to work as I say for the next three years. In exchange, you get fed, clothed, and housed with some schooling and church thrown in as a bonus."

"That ain't legal!" Hellie challenged, taking the papers.

"Read for yourself," she said, a taunting smile on her face.

Hellie looked at them. The letters that formed words that formed sentences that laid out her life for the next three years hopped around the pages like fleas upon a pillow. But she stubbornly turned each page over as though she might find something to rescue her. Finally, on the last page, she saw Harry's signature.

"Hey! That's my brother's mark!" she said, pointing to it. "That proves this ain't legal. Harry's dead! He couldn't have signed."

"Really? When did he die?"

"Been about two weeks now."

"Well, this signature was dated and notarized well over a month ago." Mrs. Gorence smiled. Her tiny face seemed so childlike, yet her eyes were so old, her voice so low. "I'm getting a little tired of this. Birdy, show these girls how to get out the back door, will you? Make sure they know how to work those machines."

"No!" Hellie said. "Harry wouldn't never have . . ."

"Well, he did," Mrs. Gorence said, breaking her off.

"What about Lizzie? She don't got no one to sign them papers."

Mrs. Gorence sighed and handed Lizzie her papers. "Look on the back page," she said.

Lizzie slowly read the last paragraph of her indenture papers. She looked at Mrs. Gorence with a quizzical expression. "This is a lie," Lizzie said, handing the papers back. "Hellie's right. This is some sort of racket. My mother's dead. She couldn't have signed those papers last month."

Mrs. Gorence propped her glasses and read, "Sarah Jane Coultrane, May 15, 1918. Notarized by William C. Ridley. Wake up and smell the manure, girls. You are both here because your next of kin agreed to send you out on that train. Fifty dollars, I believe, is the usual fee. You are both here under reduced circumstances."

"What are them?" Hellie asked.

"Poor and powerless," the woman stated.

Hellie looked at Lizzie, who looked back. "I'm telling you, I didn't sign no papers and Lizzie didn't either, and since we're the ones we're talking about for the next three years, then I say to hell with them papers and to hell with you and to hell with Harry and to hell with everyone!"

But Lizzie seemed frozen. She stared at the papers on the table, her lips fighting to hold in tears. Just then, there was a familiar wail of a neglected baby emanating from somewhere upstairs.

"And what about Joey? Where you setting him to work for the next three years?" Hellie asked.

"Don't be silly. You can't indenture an infant. But he'll grow into a good worker, even with a clubfoot. This is a big ranch. I need all the help I can get," Mrs. Gorence added. "Birdy?"

"Come on, girls," Birdy said. They were then escorted out the back door.

Hellie finally looked at Lizzie, who didn't seem to blink but just stared at the ground. "You okay, Lizzie?" Lizzie walked toward the laundry. "Lizzie?"

Lizzie walked between two crisp sheets hanging on the line. She turned and yanked down a sheet, wadded it up, and threw it to the ground. "Sold!" she screamed, now kicking the sheet. "Me thinking all this time Ma was dead!"

"Look like we was both sold out, Lizzie."

But Lizzie wasn't listening. She was pulling down another sheet, the wooden pins popping gaily into the air. She wadded a sheet and drop-kicked it. "Well, *that's* for you, Mother dear! Hope you had a good, nice long binge! Best drugs money can buy! Hope you got good and high and fell in the river and drowned!"

The back door opened and three bundles of laundry were tossed out, landing with cottony thuds on the porch and rolling down the steps. The door slammed shut.

The girls looked at the bundles and the filthy sheets lying around them, then at each other. Hellie said, "Don't you worry, Lizzie. Our kin maybe got us into this, but I'll get us out. One way or another."

Lizzie was different after seeing her supposedly dead mother's dated signature of betrayal. Hellie wasn't sure if she preferred Lizzie the Meek or Lizzie the Mad, the giggler or the grump. For two weeks she'd put up with her sullen attitude.

The best Hellie could do was keep quiet and let the washing machines and the laundry get the worst of Lizzie's anger. For two weeks, Lizzie slammed doors, kicked buckets, and actually swore out loud when she thought no one was listening.

"Dammit to hell!" she growled, after stubbing her toe on a laundry vat.

"Wow, two swear words in one sentence," Hellie said, feeding diaper after diaper into the electric wringer. The workings of the laundry had become so repetitive and automatic, that what one girl started, the other finished.

"I wasn't talking to you," Lizzie said, adding a large scoop of soap to the machine she was filling.

"Then who you talking to?"

"My toe!"

"Okay, but when you and your toe is done chatting, maybe you and me could talk about what we're going to do to get ourselfs out of this place."

"Birdy said every time a girl runs away, Mrs. G. just sends the law after her," Lizzie said, taking her shoe off to massage her toe. "We're stuck for three years. Compliments of my junkie mother and your Benedict Arnold brother."

"Well, *you* may be stuck, but I got a plan."

"You and your plans. You know what tomorrow is? Independence Day. Look how independent we are!"

Hellie looked down at her soaking skirt, her chafed, reddened hands, her bare feet. She fed the last diaper to the wringer. As Lizzie took the basket of diapers, Hellie absently added another scoop of soap to Lizzie's machine.

"You could have gotten a job in a laundry back east," Lizzie went on. "At least you'd be getting paid. Look at us. All this way across the country to wash clothes and polish silver! Some plan."

"Well, while you've been feeling sorry for yourself I've been talking to some of the hands about Pendleton." She turned on the agitator switch and sat down.

"I hate it here!" Lizzie shouted.

"Lizzie, stop it! Just stop it and listen to me! Our circumstances ain't as reduced as that old lady thinks. I got money."

"Liar."

"I do. Want to see?" Hellie indicated for Lizzie to follow her, and they padded into their back room. She hauled out her valise and pulled out the false bottom. "Look there. About a hundred bucks."

Lizzie pulled out a wad of money. "Did you steal it?"

"No, it's mine. Fair and square."

Hellie looked at the cash as she had every night since leaving New York. The edges of the bills were dog-eared from her daily counting.

"A hundred bucks could buy you a train ticket to the moon. So why are you sticking around here if you can buy yourself a ticket to anywhere?"

Hellie leaned back on her bunk and thought about it. "I reckon we'll need more than this. Providing you want out of here bad as I do. No use going from this frying pan and into the fire."

"Okay, so what's this great plan of yours?" Lizzie asked, now fanning the steaming room with a towel.

"I got something you need and you got something I need," Hellie continued.

"Go ahead."

"You know how to read and I know how to pick pockets. How's about we trade skills? Teach each other."

Lizzie stopped fanning the room and looked at Hellie. "And why would I want to know how to pick pockets?"

"Because it's clean and easy profit," Hellie said. "You learn *half* of what I can teach you, before long we'll have enough money to buy us both out of here and you can go wherever in the whole world you want. You teach me to read so's I can learn about all them places in the world."

Lizzie sat down on a stool and said, "And whose pockets are we going to pick? Each other's?" She indicated their surroundings.

"I'm one step ahead of you. Birdy says if we want, we can go to town on Sundays for church. Remember, Mrs. G. says she has to give us churching. We go to town and fill our pockets. Nothing beats Sunday-best for lead-pipe cinch pickings. And you can't tell me there ain't a nice Uncle Abe pawnbroker in all of Pendleton. One who just looks the other way. Don't worry. I can fence a train."

"I don't understand half of what you say," Lizzie said.

"You'll learn," Hellie said.

"Hellie!" Lizzie screamed, looking into the laundry room. The machine had overflowed with a huge mountain of soapsuds.

They dashed into the room and began grabbing armfuls of the suds.

"You put in too much soap, you dope!" Hellie said.

"No, I didn't!" Lizzie shouted back, turning off the machine. "You did!"

"Here, let me!" Hellie said, grabbing for a broom to sweep away the mess.

"No, I can . . . !" Swoosh! Lizzie slipped and went down. Hellie laughed so hard at Lizzie's pratfall that she nearly fell over herself.

A soaked towel in the face was her reward. "Take that!" Lizzie shouted, gathering up another wad of soaking, soapy laundry to hurl toward Hellie.

Hellie grabbed a clean diaper, twisted and snapped it. "Put it down," she warned. They circled each other; then the face-off escalated into several slippery chases around the machines, screaming at each other, laughing, scooping, snapping, and tossing suds.

Hellie took the diaper and scooped it full of suds, and, ducking Lizzie's soaking missiles, took aim. With a great windup, she tossed it toward Lizzie, who sidestepped it just as Mrs. G. was entering the room, demanding, "What is all this . . ."

Whap! Mrs. Gorence's cane flew up into the rafters as she, all ninety-eight pounds of her, went down with a faceful of soapy diaper. Her feet shot out from under her, depositing her rudely on her quite-uncushioned behind.

The only sound in the room was the washing machine still gently regurgitating rolls of suds. Then the girls realized what had just happened. It was as though they were paralyzed—frozen in time like one of Amanda's photographs . . . the soaking girls, hands to mouths, the stunned Mrs. G., eyes wide, mouth open but unable to speak.

Hellie leaped forward, but slipped and fell next to Mrs. Gorence. Lizzie rushed to help them both up, but Hellie was laughing so hard she couldn't get a firm grip on Lizzie's soapy arm, and then it was three of them on the floor, struggling to stand in the water and slippery suds.

Perry had heard the commotion and rushed in, a tide of suds creeping over his boots. He looked down and whispered a low "Uh oh."

"Don't touch me!" Mrs. G. growled as Perry leaned to help her up. Her long skirt was wet and up to her thighs, showing two bony knees and malformed legs, one enclosed in a stiff leather brace. She quickly pulled her skirt back down and said, "I can get myself up." Like a toddler, she rolled over, jutted her behind up, pushed and stood. Her salt-and-pepper hair, usually prim and organized, had come undone, and it hung lopsided and wet.

Hellie tossed a wet towel up to the rafters to unlodge her cane and caught it as it fell. She handed it to her and tried to clean off her dress. "Don't . . . say . . . a . . . word!" Mrs. Gorence said, punctuating each word. She seized her cane like a sheriff seizes a murder weapon. She pursed her lips. Hellie thought she looked like a wet stick of dynamite with its fuse only half-burned.

"You okay, Mrs. G.?" Perry asked.

Her face was stone. "No, I am *not* okay. My afterpiece is killing me." She rubbed her hip. "To say nothing of my dignity!"

"Can I get you some ice?" Hellie asked.

"No, you can *not* get me ice! Clean this mess up, clean yourselves up, and be at the house in exactly one half hour," she said. "I said I don't need any help!" she shouted to Perry as he tried to take her arm.

She turned, then came back around, reaching into her pocket. She pulled out two soaked pieces of paper and handed one to each girl. "This is why I came here in the first place. Your time sheets for the last three weeks."

She walked out, her limp more pronounced than usual, leaving little wet tracks on the porch.

Hellie looked at the papers and handed them to Lizzie. "Here. Think maybe now's a good time to start me with reading lessons." She reached into her own wet pocket and pulled out a string with a large skeleton key dangling on the end. She held it up and said, "Now, if this had been a dollar in Mrs. G.'s pocket, you and me'd be a dollar richer."

"That's the key to the silver room!" Lizzie said. "How did you . . ."

Hellie's soapy grin was all the explanation she needed.

"No! Then what?" Birdy asked Perry as they walked the path from the
horse barn to the back of the house. Hellie stopped snapping out a
filthy towel to eavesdrop.

"Then, Mrs. G. just sets there like a wet hen and about as mad, bird-
legs sprung out all about her! Thought she was going to lay an egg
right there! Then that Hellie girl offers her ice for her hindquarters! I
kept from laughing, but once I got off alone, I tell you, Birdy, I haven't
laughed so hard since Arla upset that hornet's nest in the outhouse!"
They both fell into laughter.

"Wonder what she'll do," Birdy said.

"Well, she can't send them away, I know that," Perry said. "Help's
too hard to find way out here what with the war effort and all."

All but their hair was clean and dry as the girls reported to the kitch-
en. Waiting for them were Birdy, Perry, and Mrs. Gorence. Arla, the tall,
sturdy cook, busied herself in the pantry, but glanced over her shoulder
when the meeting convened.

Mrs. Gorence sat on a pillow, wrapped in a robe, her bad leg propped
on a small stool. "How nice of you to join us," she said. "Birdy, mark
down the girls were four minutes late. While you're there, erase them
from the holiday picnic tomorrow."

Birdy went to the large blackboard on the kitchen wall that divided
the names and day's tasks and messages and made a mark in a separate

column. Then, with a swipe of the damp rag, erased the only bright spot they had on their calendar.

Hellie spotted her opening. "Ain't fair you got that writing about me and I can't even read it." She held up her time sheet. "Same with this. How do I know you ain't cheating me?"

How one small woman, sitting down, could scream and rant for five solid minutes without seeming to even take a breath, without passing out, was beyond Hellie. She had started with "If you think for one moment . . . ," crescendoed from there, and ended with "or there'll be hell to pay!" Everything in between was lost in her chorus of oaths and epithets encased in a pitch Hellie had never before associated with a little old lady.

The other adults present, used to such tantrums, just stood silent, waiting for the verbal dervish to wind down. Hellie and Lizzie stood speechless, more shocked at her outrage than chastised for the incident.

When it seemed as though she was finished, Lizzie was in tears and Hellie was gritting her teeth to keep from yelling back.

"Now, you were saying?" Mrs. Gorence said to Hellie as she daintily dotted away spit from the corners of her mouth with a lace handkerchief.

Hellie held her ground. "Lizzie's going to learn me to read and you're going to give us Sundays off."

Lizzie pulled her back, Birdy rolled her eyes, and Perry used his hand to cover his smile.

"Oh really?" Mrs. Gorence said.

"Yes. Now you and me both know good help's hard to find these days way out here, what with the war effort and all." She glanced over to Perry, who telegraphed a very slight "no" to her.

Mrs. Gorence seemed to straighten in her chair. "The key words being 'good help.'"

"We been here three weeks and not one day off," Hellie continued. "Not no schooling, not no churching, not nothing. Hell, the only fun we had ever since we been here was whapping you with a wet diaper."

"Listen, you little guttersnipe," Mrs. Gorence said, rising with a slight bobble. "You and she and that baby are here under my good graces because no one else would have you. You little rejects get sheltered and you get fed."

Lizzie brought her apron to her face and wept.

Hellie crossed her arms and said, "That indenture paper said we was to get schooling and Bible learning."

"School? Ha! There's too much work. If you think you're busy now, wait until the harvest crew arrives. I told Miss Bergeson that and she agreed. She said Lizzie already has her learning and that schooling would just bring you to ruin. But, if you insist, Lizzie can teach you to read. At night. After all your work is done. After Joey is asleep. Which is the other thing. Lizzie, you're moving into the house. Joey is too much work for Birdy, and she doesn't need to be up with him half the night."

"But I want to stay with Hellie," she said, her face red from crying and humiliation. Then, bravely, "I move into the house, Hellie moves into the house."

"Hellie will stay in the washhouse. Today's shenanigans prove to me what I have always suspected. The devil and her imp need to be separated."

"And church?" Hellie asked.

"Some of the hands hold a service in the bunkhouse. You can go there for an hour on Sunday." She stood up and steadied herself.

"I'm a Catholic and need to go to that church," Hellie said. "I already got a month behind on my confessing." That brought all eyes, including Lizzie's, to her. Hellie said it before anyone else could. "And I got a lot to confess."

Mrs. Gorence looked at her and said, "Of that I have no doubt. Very well. You may go to town when we go in for supplies and mail. On occasion. You can sit with Father Hastings while we do our errands." Then, she added with a suspicious glance, "And confess. Maybe even repent. I'm sure he'll be happy to have you sit and pray for a couple of hours in his church. It's a small church, but I'm sure it can hold all your sins."

Joey started to wail upstairs. Lizzie and Birdy were excused to tend to him. Mrs. Gorence looked at Arla and said, "And if you don't find that key to the silver room, madam, you'll be sleeping in the washhouse, too!"

Hellie fingered the key in her skirt pocket. She looked at the anger on Arla's plump face. Hellie moved toward Mrs. Gorence, barely touching her as she passed, and in so doing, slipped the key into the pocket of her robe, making sure the long string was dangling out.

"Well, what's that?" Hellie asked, pointing to the string. Mrs. Gorence slowly extracted it.

"Right there in your own pocket all along!" Arla said, taking the key and unlocking the silver room door. "All but accused me of stealing! *Madam!*"

"Don't you have work to do?" Mrs. Gorence barked at Perry, who quickly grabbed his hat and vanished.

Once they were alone, she turned to Hellie and said, "Just what makes you think you're so all-fired smart?"

"I ain't. If I was so all-fired smart, I wouldn't be here."

"I dread to imagine where you'd be if you weren't here," the old woman sniffed.

"You couldn't even begin to imagine where I'd be or where I been," Hellie said, a challenging smile coming to her face.

"Miss Bergeson said you'd be a tough one."

"Being soft gets you nothing," Hellie replied. Then, she indicated the grand house around them. "But I think you already know that. Seems to me a cripple woman shouldn't be so quick to call Lizzie a reject . . . least to her face." Hellie stared up at the jumbled letters on the blackboard. "Don't give a damn what you call me. Chances is, you're probably right and it ain't nothing I ain't been called before." She turned and they locked eyes. "But you watch what you call Lizzie. She's as good as I am bad. Why don't you mark that down on your board?"

"All right. Let's just see how tough you really are," Mrs. Gorence said, going to the blackboard and erasing the chores listed under Hellie's name. "Let's see how the tough little street arab handles fieldwork," she said. "Find Perry and tell him I want to see him."

"All that? You want me to clear out all that?" Hellie asked Perry, pointing the rake she'd been handed to the hillside of brambles and ivy and blackberry bushes. "With this?"

"Oh, no, you can use this shovel, these clippers, and that scythe," Perry said, indicating the wheelbarrow full of tools.

Hellie pulled the large scythe out of the wheelbarrow and stood it on its blade. It was two feet taller than she was. "How's it work?"

Perry took it and swept it across the weeds at his feet. "Easy as slicing lemon meringue pie," he said. "Use long, easy strokes. Watch you don't take off your foot. You'll get the hang of it."

"Or it'll get the hang of me," she said, taking it and trying to balance her small weight against the pulling swing of the scythe. She looked over the long-neglected area, not far from a pond where some horses grazed.

"What is this place?" she asked. "Some old garden or something?"

"Oh, just a spot I've been meaning to clear since I come out here, only these last dozen years. Once we get all these brambles cleared out, I can seed it and give them ol' boys some more shady grazing," he said, pointing to the horses. "They're retired. Served their time and now just out to pasture, enjoying life. So I call this the out-to-pasture pasture."

Hellie looked at the impossible task before her and said, "Thought farmers used machines these days."

"Sure we do. But Mrs. G., she wants you to do some mean, hard work, and Miss, I gotta say, this is the meanest, hardest work I can find on all the Hidden Hills."

He told her where to haul the clippings and start a burn pile and how he thought she should tackle the man-eating blackberries. He pointed to the sea of grapevines, which had grown up and now claimed the trees. Some branches of the willow trees were so entangled, it was difficult to know where the willow began and the vines ended.

"Whoever planted all these brambles way out here must have been out of his mind," Perry concluded. "And never turn your back on those morning glories or they'll get around your foot, pull you down, and smother you in nothing flat."

Hellie looked at him through squinting eyes, her old street habit of assessing someone's words. But Perry's face didn't crack into a smile. "Arla packed you a good lunch, and there's an old well and a hand pump somewheres around here. Prime it for fifteen or twenty minutes and you should get some good water."

"Prime?"

"I keep forgetting. You're a city girl. What you do is pour water from the pond onto the pump works and pump like hell. Water'll come. Eventually."

"Don't make no sense it takes water to make water," she said, propping the ancient cowboy hat Perry had given her on her head.

"Yep, just like money, huh?" Perry said, laughing. "Something else you need to know," Perry said, indicating the huge task ahead of her.

"What now?"

"Sometimes you gotta know when to plow around the stumps."

"Plow? I got to plow?" Hellie hollered.

"Just something to think about while you're up to your nose in sticker bushes."

He cocked his hat down, mounted his horse, and added, "The house is just over that hill, but don't cut through the pasture. Ol' Rumpus gets mighty territorial about his pasture."

"What about them?" she asked, pointing to the four Clydesdale retirees, now standing, shoulder to massive shoulder, watching her with curiosity.

"That's Matthew, Mark, Luke, and Lucifer. You'll figure out which one is Lucifer. Best hang your lunch on a tree branch."

Hellie looked up the hillside and thought it had doubled in size just in the time she had been standing there, vine over vine, fighting a king-of-the-hill battle for supremacy. The horses inched closer, and Hellie inched back. She'd never seen a horse that wasn't attached to a harness, under a rider, or on a plate. And these were giant horses.

"Now you just stay there," she warned them, instinctively reaching for her back pocket, making sure Slim was there. Retired or not, she figured an old giant horse could crush her worse than a young, small horse could, and she kept one eye on them as she began to plan the hillside attack.

She didn't get far. On her third step, she tripped. She went down flat, landing in a tangled mass of morning glory vines. She swore as she struggled to free her boots. The trumpet flowers popped away as she tugged at the damp vines. Mixed in the mass were young but potent blackberry vines, leaving their baby teeth in her palms.

She began her attack just before ten. By noon, she was covered in sweat and dirt. She'd unearthed the old pump and tried to resurrect it like Perry had instructed. Thirty arm-cramping minutes later, she had cool water to drink and pour over her head. Four other heads dipped down with her, anxious for a pull of cold, clean water.

"You got all that pond water!" she said, stepping back and watching the giant hooves sink into the puddle she had created with her priming. One horse sniffed the faucet, and she pumped out more water, which came in a fast, thick cascade. The horses sipped from the puddle as though they'd been waiting six years for someone to prime this pump for them.

The higher the sun rose, the slower Hellie worked. Her hands were blistered, cut, and stained. If there was muscle in her body that didn't ache, she hadn't found it. Sunburned and exhausted, she compared the mound of pulled vines and clippings to the rest of the hill—it was like her standing next to the Statue of Liberty.

Her plan was to make a path toward the top of the hill. From there, she would work east, then west. She reckoned, if she grew five or six inches, she might clear a path up the hill *maybe* by the time women got the vote or hell froze over, whichever came last.

Her appearance at the kitchen door that evening to join the rest of the domestic staff for dinner was a small miracle in itself. Never had she endured such a day. Never. Lightheaded, bloody-handed, stiff-legged, she sat down and just stared at her dinner.

The whole day was a complete blur to her. And how she had found the strength to outrun ol' Rumpus, the Brahman bull, on her shortcut home, she had no idea.

"Dis ain't no place for us, Harry," Flip whispered, glancing down the narrow alley. "Harlem ain't no place for white boys. Especially one da size of me."

"Relax. The Pope's watching over us. It's all set. It's just a drop. Besides, it's the Y." Harry boldly walked into the building, leaving the cash and taking the drugs in exchange from the black laundry attendant in the basement of the YMCA. One more successful exchange in their new partnership with the Pope and his Cardinal. A walk-off, Harry called it. Easy as pie. Their drops ranged from back doors of Fifth Avenue mansions to behind opium dens in Chinatown, and from Broadway to Harlem. Left cash, took the stuff, sold it to their dealer contact, and did it all over again and again. There never seemed to be a shortage on either end of the market.

"I tell you, Flip, it's the easiest money I ever made. Why didn't I get in on this racket years ago?" He held up a handful of bills and added, "Folks sure is dedicated to their little habits."

"Yeah, but I'm glad we're just da go-betweens. I don't like junkies. My ma and pa was both junkies. I hate everything about dem. Junkies even smell like . . . well, like junk," Flip said, pocketing his share of the take.

"Don't you wish Hellie could see us now?" Flip asked, pausing to admire his well-dressed reflection in a store window a few days later. "A couple of fancy swells, hailing a taxi just to go to Coney to see fireworks. Us! Slumming! Just like dem Fifth Avenoodles."

"She'd bust a gut laughing at that tie of yours," Harry said, pointing at Flip's diamond stickpin. "Then she'd lift that prop right off you."

"Wonder where she ended up," Flip said.

"Ah, she's got herself a sweet deal. If I know Hellie, she's sitting on velvet by now."

"Like us, huh?"

"Yeah, just like . . ."

Then, from out of the darkness, C. K. appeared.

"Well, well, well," he said, pointing to the red carnation in Harry's lapel.

"If it ain't Mr. Vanderbilt and Mr. Rockefeller."

"C. K.," Harry said, trying to count the heads in the darkness behind C. K. "You still alive?"

"No, I'm a damn ghost."

"Well, go haunt someone else," Harry said, moving ahead.

"Get 'em!" C. K. shouted to his thugs.

Harry and Flip had not lost any of their street-fighting savvy during their weeks of easy money and high living. But they were no match for the muscle in C. K.'s six-string.

C. K. stood over Harry, now bleeding and breathless, and counted the roll of money he'd taken off him. He pointed it toward Harry and said, "I figure you owe me five more bucks in interest, but seeing you bleed just about covers it." He picked up the crushed carnation that had flown off during the fight and threw it down on Harry. "I catch you or dat little sinker on my turf again, you'll wish you was dead and I'll be more'n happy to grant dat wish!"

He called his boys, and they vanished into the darkness.

"Harry . . . Harry . . . ," Flip called. "I'm hurt. Real bad. My gut. I'm hurt bad."

Harry found him and propped his head. Foamy blood oozed out of Flip's mouth. Harry picked him up and placed him on the pavement under a streetlight.

"I'm getting help, Flip. You're okay, but I gotta get help."

"Don't leave me, Harry!"

"Just to call for help."

He ran into Biff's Tavern and shouted for someone to call an ambulance. He ran back out onto the street.

"Flip!"

But Flip was dead.

31

Lizzie pulled Hellie out of a deathlike sleep—the only kind of sleep Hellie fell into since being outcast to Mount Briar, as she had named it. "Hellie! Hellie! Come on! Wake up! Today's the day!"

"Aw, go on. Evaporate," she mumbled, her New York accent punctuating her oath.

"Come on! They're going to leave without you."

Hellie sat up and got her bearings. After a month working on the hillside, her face was now tan, her hands rough and callused, her arms defined with muscle. "Huh?" she answered, looking outside to see how high the sun was.

"We get to go to town! Come on! Perry said he'd give you ten minutes to get out there!" Lizzie pulled her up and tossed her a skirt and shirt. "Get dressed. And guess what? We're going in the motor car!"

Hellie tossed on her clothes after running a wet towel over her body and dragging a brush through her tangled hair, long enough now to flirt with her shoulders, and was outside in eight minutes. She grabbed a few dollars from her stash and rushed out. Waiting for her in the Cadillac roadster were Perry, Birdy, Arla, and Lizzie.

Hellie squeezed in next to Lizzie, who had commandeered the rumble seat. "Isn't Mrs. G. coming?" Hellie asked.

"She's still under the weather," Lizzie said. "If you thought that woman was a terror sitting down, you should hear her when she's lying down! Don't know what makes that woman so mean."

Arla, sitting in the backseat, leaned toward their conversation and replied, "Nothing wrong with Mrs. G. that a strong snort now and then wouldn't fix. Step on it, Perry. I'm drier 'n Death Valley dust."

They made it to town in record time.

"What's this?" Hellie asked, looking at the large stone building.

"Catholic church," Perry replied.

"What are we stopping here for?"

"Boss's orders. Mrs. G. says you want to get caught up on your confessing. Said you get to spend the day here and I'll pick you up at four."

"But it's only nine!" Hellie protested. "I ain't spending my one and only day in town with any dang priest!"

Birdy said, "Perry, all she said was to drop her off and pick her up."

"Just decide," Arla said. "I'm way behind on my drinking time."

Hellie jumped out. "Come on, Lizzie."

"Okay," Perry said. "Now you two girls go on inside. If Mrs. G. asks me, I want to look her in the eye and tell her the truth—I saw you go into that church. And I'll want to see you come back out at four, that clear?"

"Got it," Hellie said.

"But I don't want to go to church," Lizzie said. "I'm not even Catholic."

"Come on." Pulling Lizzie up the steps, Hellie opened the church door with great, dramatic to-do. She smiled down at Perry while she bowed and scooted Lizzie through the door. She put her prayerful hands under her chin with mocking piety and waved the car off.

Once inside the darkened church, Lizzie said, "Stop it! I'm not going a step farther."

"Fine nun you'd make," Hellie said, giving her a nudge.

Hellie peeked out through the huge carved wooden door and waited to see the car disappear through a small grove of trees. "There! Let's go!" Lizzie scampered down the steps.

"May I help you?"

Hellie knew before turning around she would be facing a priest.

"No, I done my confessing back in New York."

"I see," he said with a smile that commandeered his young, pleasant face.

She started out of the door, stopped, turned, and asked, "But it's still good way out here in Oregon, ain't—isn't—it?"

His face lost its joy as quickly as it had sprung forth. "Hmm. Now let me think." Then, he snapped his fingers and said, "Yes, I believe it *is* still good, way out here. Now, why don't you run along, young lady? Your friend is waiting for you." He held the great oak door open for her.

"Thanks, mister!" Hellie said. "I mean, Mister Father."

They couldn't go anywhere in town without seeing posters advertising an upcoming event. "Go ahead. You can sound it out," Lizzie said, pointing to the first word.

"R . . . rou . . . nnn . . . dup," Hellie said, laboring over the words. "Roun-dup. What's that?"

"Keep reading," Lizzie said, taking another drink from her soda pop, which Hellie had bought.

"And . . . ha . . . haaapp . . . ee. And Happy Can—can—yon? Oh, canyon!"

"Good. Now, what's that word?" Lizzie asked, pointing. "Don't read so close. Step back if the words jiggle."

Hellie stepped back and still had to squint. "Rooo-DE-O. Ro-de-o. Rodeo. That's a cowboy show, ain't it? Isn't it?"

Lizzie said, "It starts September twelfth and goes for five days. That's about five weeks away. Maybe by then Mrs. G. will let us go, except I'll bet it costs money."

"That's the least of our problems," Hellie said. "Come on. Time for me to show you how the real Hellie Jondoe can peel a poke."

It was as easy as taking candy from a baby—only the baby Hellie marked was a young woman, pretty and well dressed and too concerned with returning the flashy glances of some men on the corner to realize that Hellie, having bumped into her, had stolen a coin purse from her bag, cunningly hung across her chest.

"So, did you see how I did that? I picked a ripe, distracted fruit. Pretty women are always distracted. One tiny little bump, a big apology, and I've annexed her hanger. Easy as dying." Hellie handed Lizzie the little purse she had "annexed." "Open it. Let's see how we scored."

Even the paralyzed side of Lizzie's face was astonished. She held the dainty little coin purse and said, "What *we* scored? You did it! Not me!" She gave the purse back to Hellie.

Hellie opened the purse and counted the coins. "Hmm, she needs to ask daddy for a bigger allowance," she mumbled. "Seventy-five cents."

"I can't believe it, Hellsbells. I thought you were just pulling my leg. I can't believe you stole that!"

"It's not stealing. I think of it as teaching."

"What?"

"Well, that sweet young customer just learned a valuable lesson. She's just learned to be more mindful of her purse and less mindful of men's attentions," Hellie said.

"But it's stealing!" Lizzie said.

"Well, if your conscience kills you, you do the blow-back. Watch. That's even funner." Hellie pulled Lizzie along toward the woman, swaying down the street.

"Lady! Oh lady!" Hellie called out. The young woman stopped.

"Yes?"

"You must have dropped this back there, lady," Hellie said, showing her the coin purse.

The woman looked a bit amazed, then inspected her purse. "Why, I wonder how . . . Well, thank you, young lady. It's not every child in these parts who would be so honest," she continued. Then, in a slight whisper, "What with all the *Indians* and *Mexicans,* you know."

Hellie nodded as though she did know. "Ma always says honesty is it's own reward. Come on, Lizzie. We're late for choir practice."

"Oh, wait," the woman said. "Here. I believe in rewarding honesty, too."

She opened her coin purse and handed each girl a quarter. "Here, and you tell your mother she's raising a fine, upstanding girl."

"Oh no, I couldn't . . . ," Hellie said.

"You can and you will. I insist," the woman said.

"Pastor Kennedy is still collecting for war orphans," Lizzie said, bringing a smile of approval to Hellie's face.

"Well, okay," Hellie said, taking the two quarters.

When the woman had gone on her way, Hellie turned and said, "War orphans?"

"I was afraid if you turned it down a third time, she'd agree," Lizzie said.

"I see your conscience is better," Hellie said.

"It's still not . . . ethical. Don't do it anymore, okay? I have a feeling they hang pickpockets in this part of the world."

Hellie said, "Come on. I hear some music. Let's see what's up."

Hellie had two dollars in her pocket when she went to town.

She had fourteen dollars when she was asked to empty her pockets at the police station.

"And you, Miss. You better empty your pockets, too," the policeman said to Lizzie.

"Yes," said the drugstore clerk who had called the police. "She's the shill. She gives you that evil eye while that other one does the dirty work."

"That's a lie!" Hellie said. "Lizzie don't got nothing . . ." But she stopped as Lizzie pulled a pair of reading glasses from her pocket.

"Ah ha!" the clerk said, pointing to the glasses.

"Those are her glasses. You can tell she's practically blind . . . ," Hellie continued, but stopped when Lizzie held them up by the telltale string with the Rexall price tag—one dollar—swaying.

"Lizzie!" Hellie said, "what the . . . ?"

"I thought they'd help you read better. You're always complaining the words are all squiggly on the page when you try to read," Lizzie explained. Then, she handed the glasses to the clerk and said, "Oh, I am so embarrassed. I promise I've never done anything like this in my whole life. I am so, so sorry. I was going to pay, but when you pulled that gun on us, well, I got all scared."

The policeman looked at the clerk, a middle-aged woman who looked more like she belonged on the business end of a piece of chalk, not a .45. "Nadine, how many times do I have to tell you to quit pulling guns on shoplifters? Someday, someone is going to get hurt."

"Do you know how many drunk cowboys I have in my shop this time of year? Like Hades I'm not packing my gun, Art." She took it off the table and put it in her purse. "Fine thing, two young girls like you.

Keep this up and you'll be working for Hattie down at the . . . *hotel*," the clerk said with a righteous snap, taking the glasses and the fourteen dollars off the table.

"Hey, you only had seven bucks in your till . . . ," Hellie said. "You can't take all that money."

"That a confession?" the cop asked.

Hellie realized her mistake and said, "Go ahead. Take it all."

"The usual charges?" the cop asked Nadine.

"Well, since I made a little profit in the deal . . . if you release them to the Witch of the Hidden Hills, that should be punishment enough, especially if you tack on some extra hefty fines. Sure would like to stay here and see her face when she finds out her new little "helpers" are nothing more than two-bit hoods, but it's after five and I got to go close up."

She pocketed her profit and left the police station. Another policeman entered the room and said, "I got her on the line, Captain."

There was a chilly silence as Captain Art Barksdale looked at his officer. "How she sound?"

"Well, let me put it this way: if she talked that way in public, I'd have to arrest her."

The captain went to a desk, picked up the phone, plastered a smile on his face, and said, "Well, hello, Scholastica . . ."

"*Scholastica?*" Hellie asked Lizzie. "What's a scholastica?"

"I think that's her first name," Lizzie replied. "Oh, Hellie, we are in so much trouble. Do you think she'll beat us?"

"She does, I'll beat her back," Hellie said. "Look, don't worry about Mrs. G. I got us into this, I'll get us out."

"Yes, yes. I know," the captain said. "Yes, very lucky, very lucky." He glanced over to the girls, sitting on a bench against a wall. "I know . . . yes . . . well, don't tell me, tell them. . . . Can't you send Perry back in to get them? . . . Okay, tell you what, on my dinner hour, I'll bring them out. Okay? Now, Scholastica, do you really want them sharing a cell with any of Hattie's girls or worse? Fine . . . yes, about six . . . and hope you're feeling better. Good-bye."

He put the phone down, sighed, and walked over to the girls. "You two just sit right there and think about what you have done. Think how lucky you are Nadine didn't press any charges. I'm taking you out to the

Hidden Hills, and you'll have Mrs. Gorence to answer to over this. And you ever so much as even *look* like you've done anything illegal in my town, you can be sure I'll . . ."

Lizzie was in tears, covering her face. If Hellie had a dollar for every such lecture she'd received from a man in a uniform, she'd be rich. She knew when to act tough, when to seem bored, and when to plead the baby act because of her youth. But none of these stances worked with Captain Barksdale.

Mrs. Gorence had situated herself in the front parlor of the grand house. She was on the couch, legs up, covered with a colorful Pendleton blanket. Perry opened the door, Arla brought in a tray of coffee, and Joey was playing on a blanket in the middle of the room, while Birdy sat next to him, stretching and manipulating his clubfoot. In all, quite the scene of domestic harmony.

Lizzie and Hellie stood, frozen, waiting for Mrs. Gorence to speak. But she didn't fly into a rage. She was chilly as she offered Art coffee and thanked him for the trouble of bringing the girls all the way out to the Hidden Hills.

"All a part of my job," Art said, stirring some sugar into his coffee. "Nice change, getting out of town. You know how heated things get in town in August. Tourists and cowboys and tourist-cowboys."

Then, he pulled out some papers from his leather case and handed them to Mrs. Gorence. "Now, these were the charges, but Nadine dropped them. But there are the usual fines to pay."

Mrs. Gorence said, "Get me my glasses and my checkbook, Birdy."

She left the room and quickly returned. Little Joey looked about for her with a concerned whimper, and Lizzie quickly took charge of him.

Mrs. Gorence signed some papers, then made out a check and handed it to Art. "I think that covers it."

He looked at the check. "Fine."

Then, she made out and ripped off another check from the large pad and handed it up to the policeman. "And I believe I have been remiss in my annual donation to the Policeman's Benevolent Fund. I hope this makes amends."

He looked at the second check and said, "Oh, yes. All is forgiven." A big smile spread across his face. "Well, I need to get back to town."

"Thank you, Arthur, for bringing the girls out. Although I think a night in jail would have been just the ticket."

"Well, they aren't bad girls, I don't think, Scholastica. You know how kids like to stab the law once in a while. I think their little foray into the world of crime is over."

Hellie looked at the policeman, then at Mrs. Gorence. "Boy, I sure learned my lesson, didn't you, Lizzie?"

Lizzie was holding Joey close, like a tired swimmer might hold a life vest. "You can say that again. I've never been so scared in my whole life. I am never, ever, ever going to do anything like that again."

"Me either," Hellie said.

Lizzie was telling the truth. Hellie was lying. And, as the eyes in the room fell on her, Hellie figured they all knew it. The fact that she had the reading glasses—Rexall tag and all—in her skirt pocket was proof of that.

Lizzie took Joey upstairs, but Hellie stayed and announced to Mrs. Gorence, "Lizzie ain't no thief."

"I know that."

"So don't you go treating her like one."

"Do you know how much your 'stabbing the law' just cost me?" Mrs. Gorence demanded. "Can you read numbers yet?" She showed her the check register. Hellie looked at it.

"How much?"

"One hundred and fifty-five dollars," she said, snapping the check-book closed.

At that, Hellie left without a word, went to the washhouse, retrieved the money in her satchel, and returned to the grand parlor as Mrs. Gorence was just hobbling out.

Hellie thunked the money down on a table and said, "There. There's eighty-five dollars. I figure I owe you . . . ," she used her fingers to count, "sixty more bucks."

"Seventy," Mrs. Gorence said, taking the money. "I can only imagine how you got this."

"No, you can't," Hellie said. "Not unless you've lived in rat holes and got food any way you could, fighting kids for a damn piece of bread. Don't matter anyhow. Money's money. And I'll get the rest before I leave this place. With interest, if you say so. And it'll be earned fair and square."

"You don't know the first thing about fair and square," Mrs. Gorence growled. "Honest living, hard working."

Hellie started to leave.

"You have not been excused," Mrs. Gorence said, raising her cane to block her exit.

Hellie stopped. "I got three more hours of daylight, I figure. I'm heading out back to work." The cane slowly came down, and Hellie added, "I make good on all I say. You'll get your money back, you'll get your three years' work out of me, and it'll all be fair and square."

Mrs. Gorence grunted with a sniff. "We'll see. We'll see."

It might have been Labor Day to everyone else in Oregon, but it was just another day to labor for Hellie. The hay harvest crews trebled the workload, making her escape from Mount Briar even more welcome.

The four retired horses now awaited Hellie's arrival into their domain. She routinely stopped at one of the barns and scooped a can of oats to busy them while she opened the gate and hauled her tools to the hillside. The heat of the day seemed to have drenched the hillside, still in full sunlight at six. The flies and bees were taking advantage of the early evening warmth and were as bothersome as they were at high noon.

She hated to admit it to herself, but she was beginning to look forward to her time on this hillside, alone with her thoughts in the seemingly mindless work. She talked out loud as she raked, clipped, pulled, tugged, and hauled, embellishing past confrontations, acting out encounters with friend and foe alike. She even started to admire the strength she was finding. She remembered other gutterpups in and out of her past when they'd go swimming and compare biceps, and offer handstands and cartwheels as shows of budding strength. The tugs of war, the king of the mountain tussles, the handshakes till one screamed "uncle," the "yeah? oh yeahs!" of one-upsmanship, and childhood dares to "step over dat line!"

Her rivals now were briars and brambles, her weapons now clippers, spades, and shovels, her gang now four old draft horses, and only one of them, Lucifer, a proper thief.

The horses followed her to the pump, where she had hauled a metal trough to give them a good watering. She filled the trough and stepped aside to let the boys drink their fill.

She took the path she'd cleared to the top of the hill and looked around. How did these things, these blackberries, grow so fast? How could a plant offer such sweet rewards at such a costly price? Didn't she clip back that thick, cruel tendril just yesterday? And now here it was again, sneaking back to reclaim the clearing atop the hill.

Having clipped off a layer from the top of the bushes, she could see what a pleasant view it was from up here. The pond below, the shady willow branches kissing the water, the browns, golds, and yellows of the horizon hills, and the back of the grand house in the distance. She dared to imagine Mount Briar in lawn and gardens and sculptured hedges like she'd seen in parks and fancy homes along her journey. Maybe swings and benches and a little fence around it—a park, she thought. A nice place for a park. Then, as though to remind her of Perry's intention for this hillside, one of the horses nickered from below.

Hellie went back to work, remembering she had only three years to get this done.

"Ow!" she hollered, dropping the long clippers and grabbing her shin. "What the . . ."

She looked down, expecting to see a large boulder hiding among the undergrowth. She tugged at the vines, grateful for the thick leather gloves that Perry had found for her. Ripe, sweet berries popped off as she pulled. A few clips and tugs and she saw it wasn't a boulder at all. She crouched down and wiped away years of moss and dirt. She squinted away the brightness of the setting sun and then tried to read.

"Mar . . . tin . . . Ann . . . annn . . . An-drew Ga . . . Ga-orence. Martin Andrew Gorence. Born Ape—April fourteen, 1893, Died May ten, 1894." Hellie looked down at the horses. "Just a baby."

Hellie tried to imagine Mrs. Gorence, the old crone, as a grieving young mother, then decided the young Martin Andrew must have been from another branch of the Witch of the Hidden Hills family tree.

The sky was a sudden, brilliant pink as the sun disappeared over the farthest of the Hidden Hills. By the time Hellie gave Rumpus the bull his handful of carrots as toll to cross his pasture, returned the tools to the shed, cleaned up, and got into bed, it would be past dark. And to-morrow, Tuesday, would bring extra laundry as the hands exchanged their dirty for clean. She wanted to get as much sleep as she could so she could work extra fast and get back here to Mount Briar and clear a view for little Martin Andrew Gorence, dead at age one.

Within a week's time, Hellie had uncovered four more graves—each one a young Gorence boy . . . William, Theodore, John, and Bryant. Each one dead before the age of eight.

"I'm telling you, Lizzie," Hellie said, as the girls worked in the large silver room off the kitchen, "there might be a whole damn cemetery up there for all I know." She made sure Birdy and Arla, working in the pantry, were not within earshot.

"Five graves? Five?"

"Well, who knows how many are up there? Each one a little kid. One of *her* kids. Dead. All died young. And get this—within just a few days of each other. What do you make of that?" Hellie whispered.

"I don't know."

"The witch probably murdered them all," Hellie said, putting a large teapot back into a gray cloth pouch and pulling the drawstring tight.

Lizzie's face went blank, her gloved hand and polish-soaked rag came down. "You think?" she said thoughtfully. Then, "You're crazy. Go on! That's plain stupid. She's no child-killer, especially her own children."

"Well, how about she *isn't* the mother? How about she's the wicked stepmother? How about she's the second wife who did away with all the Gorence children?"

"What for?"

"To inherit all this!" she said. "There's more money in this dang silver room than you and me will see in our whole, entire lifes," Hellie continued. "Jesus, Joseph, and Mary, how many tea sets can one little old lady need?" Hellie looked at the shelves loaded with bagged silver, each one with a date of the last polishing attached. She pulled down another bag, opened it, and started to polish a creamer. "Look, this isn't even tarnished."

They worked in silence, falling into the gentle rhythm of the tune Arla was humming in the kitchen.

"You know," Lizzie said, breaking the silence, "there is something . . ."

"What?"

She slowly closed the door to just a few inches. "Well, it was about a month ago. Middle of the night, and it was when Joey just got that new plaster boot for his foot, remember?"

"Yes."

"And you know how Mrs. G. says we are never to come into her rooms? How she keeps the door closed all the time and how private about that she is? Well, I heard Joey start to cry and thought I'd just give him a few minutes to get back to sleep. But he kept on, and so I got my robe on to go to him. About halfway down the hall the crying stops, and so I head back to bed. Then, I pass Mrs. G.'s room and the door's open just a bit."

Then, she used the silver room door to illustrate the story. "So I sneak over and peek in, because there's this light on. I open it just a crack, and there's Mrs. G., holding Joey and rocking him to sleep."

"No fooling? I've never seen her so much as give him a smile since we been here," Hellie said.

"And she was talking to him."

"Did you hear what she was saying?"

"Baby things, sort of. Like 'shhhsh now' and 'darling.'"

"The Witch of Hidden Hills maybe ain't such a witch all the time, then, huh?" Hellie asked.

"Oh yes, she is," Lizzie said. "Then she looks over and sees me looking in, and her hollering woke Joey and half the house. She almost threw poor Joey at me and told me to get out! get out! get out!"

They worked again in silence. Then Hellie said, "Kind of a shame, though, ain't it? No matter who them dead babies are."

"Guess I'd be mean too if I had five dead babies," Lizzie said.

Even clear out at the Hidden Hills, there had been an increasing sense of excitement as the days to the annual rodeo counted down. But Mrs. Gorence decreed that neither Hellie nor Lizzie could go to town to see any part of the Pendleton Round-Up or Happy Canyon Indian Rendezvous.

"Because," she stately flatly to Hellie's protestations, "A, you have no money, and B, because someone needs to stay here with Joey, and C, everyone else at the Hills has earned their time off. Even the haying crew put in extra hours to get their time off. And D, you both are still on probation from your last little escapade in town."

"You going to do the whole alphabet?" Hellie asked.

Mrs. Gorence pointed at the chalkboard in the kitchen. All the names had "Round-Up" under them, Lizzie's had "Joey," and Hellie's had "Air blankets, delouse beds, iron sheets."

"And I want those sheets ironed good and hot. Winter's coming on, and I want every mite and every germ killed in all the beds. Especially in the bunkhouse. With everyone gone to town, this is the perfect opportunity to fumigate. Lizzie will help you when she can. Lizzie, the doctor left new instructions for Joey's leg exercise." Mrs. G. walked away. And that was the end of the discussion.

Lizzie and Hellie watched from the bay window in the grand front room as Perry drove the car with Arla, Mrs. G., and Birdy on board. Each was wearing some version of a cowboy outfit, from boots to hat. The sun was just peeking over the eastern horizon. Two other carloads of hands had left earlier, and with each car or horse or wagon going down the road toward town, the girls fell deeper and deeper into anger.

"No fair," Hellie said. "We get the work and they have the fun."

"I don't care," said Lizzie. I don't need anyone gawking at me. I'm happy staying here." She looked at Hellie, who was staring out the window at a vanishing puff of dust on the horizon. "And you can get that out of your mind."

"What?"

"Going to town."

"I just might. Haven't decided yet." Hellie got up from the window seat and looked around the grand room. "On the other hand," she said. "We got this whole place to ourselfs. Just you, me, Joey, and about a million critters."

"Well, break out the champagne," Lizzie said, wearily. "I was up half the night with Joey, and you should see what Mrs. G. listed for me to get done today."

"Yeah, me too. So, what's the worst that can happen if we don't get it all done? What else can she take away, Lizzie?"

Lizzie stopped midstep, turned, and said, "Nothing. Absolutely nothing."

So, they agreed. Work hard until noon; then they would pack a picnic lunch, grab Joey, and enjoy that beautiful waning day of summer in some shady spot. Maybe even swim in the pond, pitch some horseshoes, chase some geese, snooze in the sun.

"Wow, you cleared all this?" Lizzie said, looking up at the partially shaved hillside.

"Mind those vines. They'll grab you, pull you down, then choke you like a boa constrictor snake."

Lizzie leaped over one, then realized she was being teased.

They had made Joey a nest in the wheelbarrow and wheeled him along. The large bonnet they had found him drooped low over his eyes, and he fussed more about not being able to see out than he did about the cast now encumbering his deformed leg.

"Grab Joey and I'll show you the graves," Hellie said, heading up the path.

One by one, Hellie pointed out the names—Martin, William, Theodore, John, Bryant.

The four horses found them, and Hellie had to convince Lizzie they were just gentle giants. "Well, Lucifer there, he'll steal anything he can get his mitts on, but them other boys are just like puppies. I'm clearing all this out to give them a shadier spot to rest."

They spread a blanket under a willow for their picnic lunch of pilfered delicacies from the pantry. Lizzie put Joey on the blanket and handed him a rattle to gum. He seemed fascinated and content to look up and see the layers of wispy green from the dancing willow. He kicked and cooed and shook the rattle.

"What's that?" Lizzie asked, pointing to a tin.

"I don't know. The label's a foreign language. But it's good because it was hid away on a top shelf. Got a picture of a big fish on it. Same with that cheese there. And look, this morning's bread and roast beef left over from last night."

Hellie spread out the picnic lunch. "And," she said, pulling a bottle out of the hamper, "since it's a party, champagne, just like you suggested."

"Oh Hellie, we couldn't! It's illegal to drink, isn't it? I mean, Mrs. G. will miss that bottle and . . ."

"And blame it on Arla," Hellie said, putting it in the pond to cool.

By two o'clock, Joey was napping soundly in the shade, the four horses were dozing close by, and Hellie and Lizzie were swinging out over the pond with a rope Hellie had tied around a high tree branch, laughing loud and long for the first time in months.

"I feel . . . kind of . . . ," Lizzie began.

"Me too," Hellie said. "I've only drunk beer before." She picked the bottle up from its watery nest and poured them each another glass.

"Am I drunk, Hellie?" Lizzie asked, sitting up a bit straighter. "Ohmygosh, I'm drunk on one glass!"

"They ought to outlaw outlawing this stuff," Hellie said. "All that—what do they call it? Pro . . . prohabitualion?"

Hellie's mouthful of consonants made Lizzie laugh hard. If it wasn't for one wizened eye casting down lifelessly, she would have a perfectly normal face. The salve Birdy had given her for her scars was working, and the sun and fresh air of the West seemed to have cleansed her skin.

"It's Prohibition," Lizzie finally got out, taking another sip of champagne. "And you're right. They ought to prohibit Prohibition!"

A thoughtful silence broke between them as they looked out over the horizon.

"You know, if it wasn't for *her* this maybe wouldn't be such a bad place," Hellie said. "I like ol' Arla. I like Birdy and Perry. Think maybe they're lovers, Birdy and Perry?"

Lizzie's eyebrow popped up, and her hand went to her mouth. "You think? They're so old! And they're not married."

"Don't know as it matters," Hellie said.

"My ma wasn't married to my pa," Lizzie confessed. Then, almost whispering, as though daring a peek around the door into her past, she added, "Now that I think about it, I sure had a lot of stepfathers and uncles. Guess my ma . . . got around."

"Least you remember your ma," Hellie said, refilling their glasses. "My ma died when I was just a little kid. But Harry said she . . . got around, too."

"Wish mine had died," Lizzie said, her voice now hard. "Spared me a lot of grief. Well, I hope she's dead by now. Maybe she'll catch that Spanish flu and die."

After her years on the street, Hellie knew that alcohol brought on three conditions—happy and sad and mad, each able to turn its back on the other in an instant. Hellie wasn't sure which to encourage. "Yeah, and leave you all her money!"

"Yes, maybe she married some rich tycoon and he dies and she gets all his money and maybe she gets the flu and dies and now I'm her sole heir and maybe some handsome Philadelphia lawyer is trying to find me right now to give me my millions!"

"You got quite a way with 'maybe,' Lizzie."

"'Maybe is all you got sometimes," she said. "Maybe my eye will grow back. Maybe I'll be pretty some day. Maybe."

"Maybe, we can find a doctor to sort of patch up your eye. Folks get glass eyes, you know. I know 'cause I won one playing marbles. Maybe someday we'll find you a doc to give you a glass eye."

"I think I stand a better chance with the lawyer and the millions," Lizzie said, looking wistfully out over the pond. She then looked at Hellie and said, "I know you're dying to know, so why don't you just ask?"

Hellie said, "I already know."

"How? I never told anybody!"

"Heard you once dreaming. Said for your ma to stop hitting," Hellie said, slingshotting pebbles into the pond to try to hit the bobbing champagne cork. "Your ma did it, didn't she?"

"Yes," Lizzie said. "She said she wanted to keep me from being pretty. Well, it worked!"

"The streets are hard on the pretty ones."

"Maybe my ma was just jealous," Lizzie said, taking the slingshot and trying to hit the cork. "Cause it happened just after . . . after that man got me."

"Pull it to your cheek," Hellie said. "Way back. Hold your arm steady."

"Like this?"

"Yeah. Now shoot. Pretend that cork's your ma."

Lizzie let the pebble go, and it nearly hit the cork. "Sink, Ma!" she called.

The girls smiled at each other. Then Hellie said, "You don't have to say any more."

"It don't matter," Lizzie said. Then, laughing, "Don't matter. Ha! I've been around you so long I'm starting to talk like you!"

"And I'm starting to talk like you!" Hellie said back. "Go ahead. Try it again," she said, handing Lizzie a handful of ammo-pebbles.

"I'm not the only one who talks in her sleep, you know," Lizzie said, taking aim again. "After we left New York you kept calling for *Archieeeee!*" She extended his name teasingly.

Hellie took the slingshot. "Here. I'll show you how . . ."

"Hellie's in love with Archie," Lizzie sang, seeing the nerve she struck.

"Lizzie, stop it!" Hellie said, standing up and going toward Joey. But Lizzie persisted with her teasing.

Hellie scooped Joey up, brushed away some grass from his cheek, and held him close. "Did you have a good little nap, buddy?" she asked him.

"Hellie and Archie, sitting in a tree, K-I-S-S-I-N-G . . ."

"Lizzie, shut up!" Hellie screamed, bringing a loud startled screech from Joey. Lizzie's face went blank as Hellie worked to calm Joey. "That's okay, buddy, I wasn't yelling at you."

"Okay, I guess maybe you aren't in love with Archie," Lizzie said, also a bit startled. "I was only . . ."

"Archie's dead," Hellie said.

"Oh, Hellie, I'm sorry. Was he . . ."

"Nope, and what's more, I killed him."

Lizzie smiled and said, "Oh, right. Died of a broken heart?" She looked at Hellie, now staring icily out over the pond. "Oh, you're not joking."

Hellie turned and said, "It was self-defense. I shot him with his own gun. Him and me were fighting over the gun. Doesn't matter. He needed killing. He shot my brother and . . . Well, Archie's dead, Harry's dead, and I don't give a damn about either of them. Here, it's your turn to change Joey."

Hellie and Lizzie sat on the grand front porch way past dark, carefully releasing more hints about their troubled and violent pasts. The coffee and the conversation helped to return them to sobriety.

"You think they're going to spend the night in town?" Hellie asked, looking toward the faint glow on the horizon that was Pendleton.

"Who knows?"

"Wonder what's all so special about a rodeo," Hellie said. "Perry said folks come from all over to watch it. Who wants to see horses and cows jumping all over the place?"

"Well, there's other stuff. Games, parties, carnival. You know, sort of circus stuff. Big parade the last night. Perry said there were five thousand people at last year's parade."

"Five thousand?" Hellie echoed. "Wow, that's at least ten thousand pockets!"

"Hellie, don't you even dare think about that business again! You're lucky we're not rotting in the Pendleton Jail for Wayward Girls."

"Well, at least we might be able to see some of the parade on Sunday," Hellie said. "Don't look at me that way! I'm not thinking what you think I'm thinking."

"Okay, then what are you thinking?"

"I'm thinking we should do something special, you know, an extra project, something that makes her happy and gets us on her good side."

"She's never happier than when we're miserable," Lizzie said. "My head hurts. Does your head hurt?"

"She said everyone puts in extra hours to get time off for Round-Up," Hellie said, pouring Lizzie more coffee from the fine silver service.

"I don't care about Round-Up. I like it here having the place all to ourselves."

Hellie was looking down the driveway. The three hooded overhead lights cast a friendly warmth on the rows and rows of raspberry bushes that lined part of the long drive. The leaves had turned yellow, as though they were slowly pining away after the harvest of their summer-long labor. Behind the arbor was an old sun-bleached picket fence, seemingly holding in nothing more than a memory.

"I think I have an idea."

The idea was to dismantle the old picket fence and rebuild it around the small little graveyard Hellie had uncovered in the "out-to-pasture pasture." They worked that Friday and Saturday, after the crews had left for Round-Up, after they had double-timed it to complete their own chores. They dug fence-post holes, and hammered, tied, and wired the rickety pieces together with anything they could find in the barns.

While Hellie whitewashed, Lizzie glued and wired grapevines together until they formed a lacy "G" inside a web of twigs that became a little gate. Lacking hinges, they set the gate with strips of old leather reins, salvaged from the tack room.

The final touch was a spring wagon seat, detached from a lame, lopsided, and useless buggy found encased in cobwebs in one of the barns. They hauled the seat to the graveyard and placed it so one could look out over the pond.

"Well," Hellie said, sitting on one of the gravestones and looking around the enclosure, "I think we did it."

"Not bad, Hellsbells," Lizzie said, walking a slow circle, inspecting their work.

"That gate is beautiful," Hellie said. "You have talent."

"Sure, there is such a need for lady gate-smiths," Lizzie said, scooping Joey up. "When you going to start walking?" she asked him, holding him high in the air and then nuzzling him.

Hellie said, "Think that cast will make it harder for him to learn to walk?"

Lizzie said, "Well, who knows? Doc and Mrs. G. fight about it. Wait and see, I guess."

Both girls had come to adore Joey's giggle, and they competed to see which of their names was going to be his first word. Hellie said, "I think Perry needs to make him that special shoe Birdy talked about. That's why he's not walking. He can't walk in that cast. His foot probably hurts to put weight on it."

"Mrs. Dough Bug's got more money than God. You'd think she'd get him to a special doctor. Not that Doctor Quack Cornell," Lizzie said.

"Quack?"

"That's what Birdy calls him—Quack Cornell. Come on. I still have that fruit cellar inventory to do."

"Well, no one asked you to!" Mrs. Gorence screamed. "This is none of your business! I don't even want you up here!"

Hellie and Lizzie's faces of delight were quickly crushed by her reaction.

"But, Perry, he wanted me to clear out . . . ," Hellie started.

"Perry! What's he have to do with this?"

"Nothing. He just told me to clear this area out for the horses and then I found . . . well, I didn't want the horses to step on the . . ."

"Has Perry seen this?" she demanded, pointing a long, slim finger toward the little graveyard.

"No, just Lizzie and me."

"We worked extra fast on our chores and then spent all weekend setting this fence and painting and . . . the carriage seat . . . and everything . . . ," Lizzie tried, her good eye magnified with tears. "Hellie wanted to go to Round-Up . . ."

"And it was you what wanted me doing hard work, remember?" Hellie said, her own temper rising. "Tough work for the little street arab!" She showed Mrs. Gorence her scarred, callused hands. "Look! You think I got these polishing silver?"

Mrs. Gorence took the gate and tried to pull it off. "Get rid of all this! You hear me? Tear it all down!"

"We thought you'd be pleased!" Lizzie wailed. "We thought it would make you happy."

"Well, you thought wrong!" Mrs. Gorence snapped, yanking the gate off its leather hinge and stepping on it, crushing the latticework Lizzie had worked so hard gluing together.

Hellie pulled on Mrs. Gorence's arm. "Stop it! Lizzie made that special for you! Did you even see the 'G' she put together with twigs?"

"Listen to me, both of you ungrateful little bastard brats! You are here for one thing and one thing only: to work as I say! You are nothing more than my servants! You aren't to 'think'! You aren't to go where you aren't wanted!"

Lizzie was on the ground, trying to pull together pieces of the gate, crying helplessly and rocking the broken pieces in her lap, as lovingly as she would rock her doll or little Joey. She stood up and said, "I'm sorry. I didn't mean . . ."

Mrs. Gorence slapped Lizzie across the face. "And you aren't to speak until you're spoken to!"

Hellie whirled Mrs. Gorence around and held her close to her face. "I don't know about them five babies in the ground there, but God must have known what he was doing, taking them away from the likes of you!"

"Hellie, don't!" Lizzie sputtered. "It's okay, it's okay . . ."

Mrs. Gorence raised her fist to strike Hellie, but Hellie caught it and easily forced it down. "See how tough this bastard brat's gotten?" she growled. "Don't you never strike Lizzie again!"

Mrs. Gorence stood assessing Hellie, rubbing her wrist.

"Now, maybe it's time to give us back our indenture papers. Lizzie and me are going to work this hard, might as well be for wages and respect," Hellie spit, throwing the crushed gate onto one of the now-manicured graves.

"Not on your life," Mrs. Gorence said, a small little smile crossing her tight lips. "I wouldn't dream of breaking up our loving little family." She turned to leave, but added over her shoulder, "I want that fence torn down so the brambles grow back. And you're not to come here again."

"I mean it!" Hellie screamed after her. "Lizzie and me want our freedom!"

Mrs. Gorence turned and screamed back, "June eighteenth, nineteen hundred and twenty-one! Mark your calendar!"

Hellie jerked up a section of fence and hurled it down toward Mrs. Gorence. "Fine! These dead babies don't mean nothing to me! Let the brambles take 'em!"

"That's what I had in mind when I seeded this ground!" Mrs. Gorence yelled over her shoulder.

"You what?" Hellie demanded.

"Hellie!" Lizzie cried, pulling Lizzie's arm. "You'll only make things worse."

They watched the old woman limp down the path toward the little dray Perry had hitched up to bring her out for the visit.

They slowly started to dismantle the fence they had worked so hard building the two previous days. One by one, the old, retired horses came to investigate, now that the screaming was over.

"Here you go, boys," Hellie said. "All yours."

They looked at the area, but only Lucifer seemed interested in the little graveyard. He gave the crushed gate a curious sniff, then turned and lumbered after the other three down to the pond.

Section by section, the girls tossed their makeshift fence pieces into a pile.

Lizzie looked at the freshly whitewashed pickets, now lying crisscross like pickup sticks. "Sometimes I wish I was as tough as you. Seems like you're always coming to my rescue."

"You're tough, Lizzie. You just don't know it yet."

"Yeah, tough as eiderdown. I wish I could be more like you. I don't know—people start screaming and hitting and I . . ."

"Never mind, Lizzie. You're the smart one. I'm the tough one. Smart and tough makes for a good double-team. Maybe between the two of us we can figure a way out of this."

"What about not jumping from the frying pan into the fire?" she asked.

"Well, I figure, it's hot either way."

They finished with the fence, bid the five small graves good-bye, patted Matthew, Mark, Luke, and Lucifer, and made their way back to the house just as the mid-September sun set on the Hidden Hills.

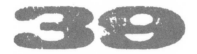

Harry knew he'd do better as a solo. He missed Flip, but had his own interests—and those of the Pope—to look after. As more and more soldiers returned maimed from the battlefields in Europe, the more he was able to expand his trade. Demand was up, supply was down, and prices skyrocketed.

By early October, he was set. Money in the bank and a set of rooms uptown, respectable folks for neighbors. He'd even tried to better educate himself by reading everything he could get his hands on and using a thesaurus and a dictionary to help him. Someone at the track had told him an uneducated man with money is a bum-to-be, and he had never forgotten that. One had to be able to read more than tote boards, racing forms, and street signs.

To his own surprise, he became an avid reader and prided himself on being able to read the newspaper and learn about world affairs, not the least of which was the war in Europe, the war that, indirectly, provided so well for him that summer.

The drop was late that day, and Harry had time to find a park bench and smoke a cigarette in a sunny spot. Someone had left the *New York Evening Journal* on the bench, and Harry used it to hide his face while he watched for his connection over the top of the paper. He perused the want ads, always interested in the sort of things people were getting rid of and the sort of things people were looking for. He read the obituaries and counted the war dead for the week. Gimbels was having a sale on winter coats, and a new jeweler who specialized in men's watches was opening not far from his apartment. All good things to know.

He especially liked photographs in the paper, and his eyes always wandered to those first . . . like a child who still prefers picture books to actual reading books. So the article's title went unnoticed. What Harry did notice was the intense, wide-eyed, I-dare-you-smile of Hellie.

He sat up straight and quickly turned the page, where he saw three more photos of Hellie and a strange-looking girl whose hair covered half her face. He read a caption. Couldn't be—but it was. The girls were identified as Helena and Elizabeth—no last names. He read the article as fast as he could, but many of the longer words were foreign to him.

He seized the paper and asked a woman on an opposite bench, "Pardon me, ma'am, could you tell me what this here word is? I forgot my specs."

The woman said, "Well, let me get out my own specs." She pinched them on her nose and looked at the word over Harry's well-manicured fingernail. "Indenture," she read.

"Ah," Harry said. "Indenture. As in . . ."

"Well, as in . . . you know. If you are indentured, you are conscripted, I guess."

"Drafted?" Harry asked.

"Well, no. A person can sell themselves, sort of," the lady said.

"Sell? Like slavery or something? That legal?"

"I guess so. I read that article too, son. It's more about finding good work for the orphans. People provide room and board—you know, a home, sort of—to have them work for a certain amount of time. If I recall, those two girls are sent out for three years. It's really quite scandalous, if you ask me. No telling who might take them or what they might want them to do . . . well, I'm sure you've heard of white slavery. It's a disgrace how we treat our orphans, isn't it?" She took her glasses off, signaling the end of the conversation. She called for her nanny to gather up her children.

"Yes, it is. Thanks."

He read the article three times, then tore it out and pocketed it just as he saw his drop arrive. He didn't even count the money this time. He had other things to do—not the least of which was to find the address of the person who wrote the article—one A.B.E. Collier.

Harry called the phone number listed on the masthead of the newspaper. Until that moment in time, it never occurred to him that there
were people behind stories, that someone sat at a desk and wrote, that
others went out and took photographs. The wonder of a newspaper
had never once occurred to him—other than sports scores and crimes
stories and the occasional obituary, like the one he had paid to be written for Flip.

After some charming wrangling peppered with lies, he learned the
address of Collier's office from the phone lady at the newspaper office.
He hung up and headed for Greenwich Village and the studio of A.B.E.
Collier, Photographer-Journalist.

Like everyone else, he was first taken aback when he learned A.B.E.
Collier was a female. She had a small front office, a wall displaying her
formal photography, a darkened studio in back, and stairs that went
presumably up to her apartment.

"Hellie's *brother?*" she asked, the pencil slipping from her hand.
"*Harry?*"

"The same, and I'd be grateful if you'd tell me where I can find her."

"But she said you were dead."

"Oh," Harry said, wiping away a boyish smile. "Change of plans. I
mean, well, it's a tragic story. And it's family business anyhow."

She sat down in the sagging wicker chair behind the small desk.
"Good. Because tragic family stories sell newspapers." She sneezed, he
blessed her, then explained more about the tragic life of himself and
Hellie.

He left out the evil elements—their life of crime, the shootout with
Archie, and the fifty dollars he'd received from the Society for Friendless Children. "So, I had to get Hellie out of the city. And see, since then,
well, I come into some money and I'm thinking, reading your article
and all, I'm thinking I done Hellie wrong and I got to get her back. We're
each other's only kin."

"Some rich relative die and leave you money?" she asked. "You look
a bit young to have made your mark in business or on Wall Street."

"I make my own mark," Harry said coolly, and turned the conversation back to Hellie. He pointed at the photo of the girls at the train
depot. "So where was this last picture taken?"

"Like it says in the article, a small town in Oregon. That's all I can tell you. She and that other girl, Lizzie, got placed out there. And Oregon is a long, long way from the Bowery."

"She don't look too happy," Harry said, looking at all the Hellie and Lizzie photos Amanda had brought out to show him.

"No, she was still mourning her dead brother," she said, with a cool snap to her voice.

Harry looked at her. "Hellie never would have got on that train west if she thought I was alive. Hellie ain't the type to turn her back on no one. I had to let her think . . . look, none of this is your business anyhow and . . ."

"Well, in case you're racked with guilt over Hellie, I will at least tell you this: She was placed with a very wealthy rancher. So maybe you dying was Hellie's good fortune after all."

"You mean she got herself a rich family?"

"Yes, aren't you thrilled for her?"

"What about that indenture thing?"

"I'm sure a girl like Hellie can make the best of things," Amanda said, lighting a cigarette and coughing. She put it out and said, "Time to quit."

"You mean like Rockefeller rich?" Harry persisted.

Amanda watched Harry as he spoke, then interrupted him. "Curiouser and curiouser," she said.

"What's that supposed to mean?"

"You know, in a way, I owe Hellie a debt of gratitude. Not only did the Hearst papers buy this story, but they have asked me to do a follow-up," Amanda went on. "In a way, I owe Hellie and Lizzie a part of this advance." She opened a desk drawer and pulled out a check paper-clipped to a contract. "I wasn't sure I wanted to make another trip out west this time of year. But having you just show up here—alive, no less—adds a certain, well, dramatic angle to the piece. Maybe it's just too serendipitous to pass up."

Harry blinked at her. She added, "Maybe it's my lucky day. Maybe I can turn this exposé into a piece about family and home and belonging. With all the horrid war and influenza news, we need more happy endings."

Harry looked down at her and said, "I don't got one clue what you're talking about, ma'am. What's the war got to do with Hellie and me?"

Amanda stood up and tapped her lip with her pencil and said, mostly to herself, "What an angle. Harry, I have a proposition for you . . ."

"No angles, no propositions."

"How about I take you to Hellie?"

"How about you just tell me where to find her? I'll even pay you. How do you like *that* angle?"

"They say a picture is worth a thousand words. Well, it's also worth a thousand bucks." She tapped the uncashed check and the Hearst Corporation contract. "Maybe more if I can capture Hellie when she sees you alive."

Harry thought, absently jingling the change in his pocket.

"Oregon's a very big state," she added with a taunting smile.

They locked eyes. "I can get that Society for Friendless Children to . . ."

"Like it says in my article, Harry, they seal the records. They wouldn't tell Woodrow Wilson a thing about Hellie's placement. Trust me. I know that outfit. I did my research."

"So the only way I can find my sister is for you to take me? So's you can write up more about Hellie and take some pictures?"

"Seems like a reasonable exchange."

Harry was now looking at the photographs and framed article on the wall from the *Evening Journal* piece. He turned and said, "Look, if you want to write up some more about Hellie, then I don't care. That's up to her. But you keep my mug out of your story. That clear? Not one photograph, not even one word describing me, that clear?"

"Why? Afraid someone will recognize you?"

"Never you mind why. That's my business."

Amanda assessed his expression and the tone in his voice. "Agreed. I won't even use your name. When can you be ready to leave?"

"I got some business to finish up. Gimme three days."

"Good. Three days. Gives me a chance to kick these sniffles. Pick me up here on Monday, October seventh. Eight a.m. The Chicago Limited leaves Grand Central weekday mornings at ten."

He put his hat back on, shook her hand, and said, "Deal. Monday. Here. Eight o'clock in the morning."

40

Harry looked about his set of rooms and poured himself another whiskey. Now that he worked a better racket, he could afford a better bootlegger. He looked at his new gold watch, downed the last of his drink, pulled on his tailor-made suit jacket, and buttoned his spats. He had an appointment to keep down at Coney.

Harry loved Coney Island—the lights, the gaiety, the constant movement and noise, the distracted crowds, the pretty girls who strolled along the boardwalk on a sunny Sunday, flashing their eyes for a quick flirtation.

Harry had been too occupied that summer to spend much time soliciting those same flirtations. Besides, his own dangerous charms were no match for the uniformed soldiers. Always, always, the girls smiled the sweetest to the soldiers, and Harry was getting to the age and size that made women wonder why he *wasn't* in a uniform. After all, America was at war.

But this Sunday Coney outing was strictly business.

Harry immediately noticed something was different on the boardwalk. It was a crisp, beautiful fall day. Where was the crowd? He looked at his watch—noon. Where were the after-church people? The hordes of returning soldiers out making up for their months in the trenches of war?

Two women passed, each with gauze masks dangling off their necks, like they were merely touting the latest fashion. Then he remembered the posters he'd seen about town. Not the war posters, but the influenza posters listing ways to prevent the spread of germs. How a tiny influenza germ could somehow sail across the ocean and make people cover their faces and hide away in their homes on a beautiful fall Sunday was beyond him.

He looked at the short lines at the concessions. Where were those high-pitched shrills of delight mixed with the come-hither bark of pitchmen, all gently muted by the ocean?

Still, the salt air mixed with the smell of fresh popcorn and oversteamed hot dogs reminded Harry of childhood days when he and Hellie would eat their fill at Coney and, between stealing and looking pitiful, never spend a dime. Harry bought himself an ice cream cone, sat on a picnic table, and waited.

He appeared from behind. "Make it fast, son. Her meter's running." Harry turned to see the Pope and a flashy woman next to him. "This is Sophia. Here, honey, here's a fin. I got business to discuss. Buy yourself some frilly or a roller-coaster ride."

The woman, black as midnight and dressed in gaudy golds, took the five dollars, placed it between her generous cleavage, and walked away with a regal sway.

The Pope folded his arms and said to Harry, "You know I don't like telephone calls on weekends. This better be important." He was nattily dressed and looked like he was fresh out of Harlem's best clubs. Hardly the yas'sir–yas'am orderly Harry had first met in the hospital.

"It is. Look, Pope, I got some business I got to do."

"What kind of business?"

Harry had prepared for the Pope's questions. "Got me another grift out west," he said, trying to match the Pope's tone. "I'll be gone for a few weeks. Thought I'd . . ."

"You walkin'?"

"No, no, of course not. I just need to tend to other things for a bit."

The Pope fingered the lapel of Harry's new suit. "I see you're gettin' real used to the finer things in life." He looked around. "Where's your shadow? Flash? Zip?"

"Flip," Harry said. "I told you, he got killed."

The Pope nodded his head, his jaunty bowler dipping as he did. "Oh yes, I remember. Took a knife in some brawl, right?"

"That has nothing to do with us, Pope. That was some other score."

The Pope looked out over the small regatta of moored boats, bobbing up and down on the choppy surface. "Cops took him away. You claimed him. I hear some gang's looking for you. The hell it don't have nothing to do with our arrangement."

"That was back in July. The heat died long ago," Harry said.

The Pope took Harry's ice cream cone and devoured the entire top scoop and mushed the creamery, then tossed the cone into the ocean below, where seagulls were quick to start fighting over it.

"You see that right there," the Pope said, chocolate seeping out of his mouth. "See them birds, how they all fight over that?" He took the crisp silk scarf out of Harry's coat pocket and wiped his face with it, then tossed it after the cone, now floating in fragments. He looked at Harry and added, "What one bird don't get, another will."

"Look, I didn't come here to talk about Flip and I sure as hell didn't come to talk about birds," Harry said, reasserting himself.

The Pope waved his large, well-manicured hand and said, "Well, that's all you are to me, boy, just some bird fighting for a bit of something I toss your way."

"I'm leaving tomorrow, but I'll be back in two weeks, tops."

"You forget about that shipment I've been working on with the Cardinal?"

Harry paused. He had forgotten. "Of course not. I just thought you could, well, maybe hold off a few weeks."

The Pope laughed. "And what? Just have the Cardinal keep the junk in his damn locker at the hospital? You *are* green, aren't you?"

"Well, turns out I got pretty big prospects out west now all of a sudden."

"You amputate now, you walk for good. Plenty of chumps I can get to make drops."

Harry pulled the Pope by his arm. The Pope glared at his hand, and Harry quickly let go. He stood back, set his jaw, and said, "Say, whose idea was this racket?"

The Pope smiled. "You're just a stooge, kid. One of dozens I got. I can get any cheap hood to stooge for me. Go peddle your papers out west."

"You don't get it, Pope. I'll be back. Gimme two weeks, maybe three," Harry said, now following him toward the merry-go-round. Its calliope music nearly drowned out his words. "Pope, you know I wouldn't leave if it didn't mean a big score."

That caught the Pope's interest. "How big?"

"I won't know till I get there. But when I come back I'll have the kind of dough we need to get that speedboat you were talking about. Maybe two. You said you wanted a slice of the rum-running market."

Sophia had appeared, holding a cone of bright pink cotton candy, a wisp of the confection daintily held between two fingers.

"You saying you'll have cash to invest?" the Pope asked as Sophia popped the cotton candy into his mouth.

"I'm saying I want a partnership," Harry said.

The Pope mouthed the candy, held his arm for Sophia, and said, as he turned to walk away, "Have a good trip, son. Write. But only if you get work."

Harry got a cab and was knocking on the locked door of A.B.E. Collier's studio at 8:00 a.m. on the nose. A light came on from the back room, and he heard feet padding toward the door. The bolt unlocked and the door opened a few inches.

"Yes?" a woman asked.

"Miss Collier said to pick her up at eight. We have a train to catch."

The door opened another inch, and the woman, old, stout, and worn, said, "Who are you?"

"Look, she here or not? Did she already leave for the station? Just tell me so I can get there myself."

He tried to look into the studio, but the woman was adamant to keep him out. "No, stay outside."

"Oh, I get it. She changed her mind. Typical dame. Well, then just let me talk to her. It's about my . . ."

"Wait one minute," she said, closing the door.

Harry tried to peek through the curl of the pulled-down window shade. The woman came back and opened the door. "Are you Harry?" she asked.

"Yes. Say, what's going on here?"

The woman stepped outside the door, closing it behind her. She handed him a letter. "If you're Harry, then this is for you. There's a case inside the door, too."

Harry looked at the envelope with his name written on it. "Can I just see Miss Collier?"

The woman sighed, then said, "No. I'm afraid you can't. Miss Collier died about three o'clock this morning. I'm sorry."

It was then Harry noticed the woman's white uniform under her heavy black cape, a Red Cross badge on her pocket peeking out.

"Died? But I just saw her a few days ago. She wasn't sick. She just had a cold. How could she be dead? What happened here?"

"I'm sorry, son," the nurse said, glancing at the watch on a chain around her neck. "If you are a close friend, I could allow you upstairs to view the body, but really, I don't advise it. This flu doesn't leave a kind calling card. Such a shame. She was a pretty woman."

"But I don't understand," Harry said. "Then what's this?"

"She had me write it for her yesterday when she knew she wasn't going to make that train. Something about, oh, I don't remember. I've taken down so many deathbed letters and wills. Even a few confessions. I usually just tear those up. That one's about, oh, your sister. Millie, I think."

"Hellie?"

"Yes, that might have been it. Read it yourself. And here, come inside to get that case. I'm too tired to move it. I've been up all night, and I have four calls to make today."

She taped a piece of paper to the door. All it said was "FLU DEATH."

She opened the door, showed Harry the leather case, sealed closed with straps. He took a quick look around the darkened room, a furtive glance toward the light from upstairs where Amanda Collier lay dead of what, Harry wondered, the sniffles?

The faces from the photographs on the walls seemed to stare back at Harry as though to ask, what happens to *us* now? He saw the one of Hellie, sitting atop a rack of luggage, looking hard and defiant, staring at the lens as though daring it to come one inch closer, Slim the slingshot balanced on her knee. He took it down off the wall.

"Come on. Out with you," the nurse said, holding the door open for him. "Leave it unlocked. For the undertaker."

"But what about . . . didn't she have family or . . . ?"

"If she did, she never once mentioned them and no one came to see her, either. Just wanted me to get that note and case to you. Come now, come on out. Nothing left in there but germs and ghosts."

He hauled the case out of the door and closed it. He looked around, shocked and confused, saw the taxi driver looking warily at the sign on the door, then said, "Can I drop you someplace?"

"Where are you heading?" she asked back, consulting a slip of paper with the address of her next call.

"Grand Central, I guess."

"Nope, I'm heading the other direction. Thanks, anyway." She handed him a gauze mask. "Here. Take this and my advice: wear it if you're riding a train. And sit by an open window." She lifted her own small valise and started walking away. She turned and said, for the first time with a kind smile, "I'm sorry, Harry. I'm sorry for your loss. I'm getting far too callous. I forget sometimes. Really, my condolences."

She turned and left.

Harry looked blankly at the mask—the latest fashion—then got into the waiting taxi.

"Where to?" the driver asked as he pulled up his own mask.

"I'm not sure," he said, the shock of the morning still setting in. He opened the envelope, and a long train ticket fell out. He read down through the stops and train changes until his eyes landed on the final destination. "Pend-al-ton," he read out loud. "Pendleton, Oregon."

"This cab don't go that far, Mack," the cabbie said.

Harry glanced up at the second story over Amanda Collier's studio. "Oh," he said absently. "Well, then Grand Central."

"That I can do," the cabbie returned, slipping the car into gear.

Harry had to ask the cabbie to speed it up so he could make the train. It wasn't until he was aboard, trying to look as though he knew what he was doing, and settled into a seat, that he pulled out the note the Red Cross nurse had given him.

In Amanda's steady hand, it read:

> My dear Mr. Jondoe;

He looked across the aisle and smiled—Jondoe—his pet name for Hellie and himself. Hellie must have been using that name.

> If you are reading this, I will have gone to my reward, although I remain doubtful of the riches therein.
>
> Please see to it that your sister gets the enclosed envelope and the case. I am leaving Hellie a camera, tripod, and some books. She showed an interest in photography. Anyone who views the world as she does will have a keen, artful eye. I would love to have seen things from her point of view.
>
> Please find Hellie and make sure she gets these things. Here is my own train ticket to Pendleton, Oregon, and you can . . .

Then, in parentheses:

Sir; Miss Collier is no longer able to speak. As her nurse, I will close this letter for her as she closed her previous letters dictated:

Sincerely,
Amanda B. E. Collier, Photographer-Journalist

"Pardon me. This seat taken?" a young man asked, looking at the valise on the seat opposite Harry. Harry had had the facing seats to himself since changing trains in Chicago.

"No, no," Harry said, pulling the valise away. "Anything for our boys in uniform."

"Thanks," the soldier said, tossing his duffel in the overhead rack and taking the seat. "But in exactly one week, I will be an *ex*-boy in uniform."

"Getting out, huh?"

"Yep. And none too soon," he said, offering Harry a cigarette. "It's French. My last pack."

"I don't want to take your last . . ."

"No, please. They're horrible! Too, well, *French* for me. Kind of sissy, if you know what I mean," he added with a genial laugh. "See for yourself." He struck a match and lit Harry's cigarette.

"I see what you mean about these fags." Harry's grimace made the young soldier laugh. "Nothing but smoke. So, you saw action in France, huh?"

"Yep, killed six Krauts before one gave me this little going-away present," he said, lifting a pant leg and showing Harry a leg with half the calf muscle missing.

"Sorry," Harry said, grimacing politely.

"Aw, it's not so bad. They give me stuff for the pain. It's not so bad."

Harry looked at the soldier and figured he was probably just a year or two older than him . . . eighteen and already to war and back.

"Billy Tucker," the soldier said, offering his hand.

"Harry . . . Jondoe."

"So, you don't sound like you're heading, well, home. You sound like you're maybe from . . . ?"

"Yeah, New York," Harry said, knowing his thick Bowery accent would always announce his origins. "Good to know you, Billy."

They exchanged polite pleasantries—Where you heading? What's the weather like? Did you see that good-looking dame in the fur coat?

"What sort of work are you in?" Harry asked, trying to keep the conversation on Tucker and not himself.

"When I'm not putting Krauts in the ground, I'm putting others in the ground."

"How's that?"

He leaned close and whispered, "I'm an undertaker. And between you and me, what with the war and that flu, this is *the* business to be in. If you have money to invest, buy stock in your local undertaker."

Harry smiled and finished his cigarette. Eventually, each young man drifted into a quiet slump, watching the Wyoming countryside glide by. The soldier fell asleep, his head slipping onto his chest where his chin gently touched his Purple Heart medal.

The soldier began to cough, pulling him awake. Embarrassed, he apologized to Harry. He seemed to twitch a little as he looked at his watch. He then excused himself, asking which direction the men's lavatory was. Harry pointed to the car behind them.

He didn't see the young soldier again until the train stopped in Pocatello, Idaho, when he limped back into the car to retrieve his grip.

"This is my stop," he said, offering his hand to Harry. "Sorry I wasn't very good company. Ended up talking to that fur-coat woman in the dining car." He sighed, then added, "Sure am going to miss this uniform."

"No need to explain," Harry said. "Dames always come first, huh?"

The train jerked to a stop, and the soldier lost his balance and Harry rose to steady him.

"Well, good luck to you. Hope you land that big railroad deal."

"Thanks," Harry said. "Hope you get that job back."

The soldier patted his Purple Heart. "My sarge used to say a uniform is a job and every medal is a raise, and an injury . . . ," he tapped his leg, "is a promotion."

Harry knew from the soldier's sloppy speech, his goofball grin, his lack of eye-to-eye focus, his slow, full-of-junk sway, that he was taking morphine for the pain.

He swallowed hard, remembering his own brief encounter with the cooling chemical as it snaked through his veins, scooping away first the pain and then even the memory of the pain. He wondered what the morphine traffic was in a town called Pocatello, in a state that claimed potatoes as their gold.

He looked down at the wallet he had lifted when the soldier had lost his balance, opened it, and pocketed the cash. He gazed at the hazy photo of the soldier's parents, tossed the wallet out the window, then went to the dining car to find the fur-coat woman.

Like Hellie before him, Harry cased out Pendleton as any street arab cases out the new and exciting possibilities of a different turf. He stood on the train platform and closed his coat against the chill of the fall evening. This was the same spot, he recognized, that Hellie had stood in the photograph. The town laid out sleepily before him, showing no signs of opportunity or excitement or Hellie.

He had put some thought into finding her while journeying west. If he knew Hellie, she had already made a small name for herself. And she was with some rich rancher. How many of those could there be in a town this size? But he was exhausted, having slept curled up on a seat each night, rather than spending the money on sleeping accommodations. His neck was sore, and he felt the restless ache of being confined to a passenger car.

First and foremost was to obey his dry throat screaming for a cold beer. The universal flash of a window light beckoned to him to the Rainbow Cafe two blocks away.

He walked into the Rainbow, and immediately all eyes were upon him, cowboys all. He reminded himself he was just as out of place here as a white boy in Harlem, three thousand miles east of where he now stood, smiling as he took his derby off.

"Hello," he said to the man behind the bar, taking a stool. Two old men at the corner of the bar acknowledged him. A grease-stained menu was plopped down in front of him.

"Oh, no. Just a beer, thanks."

"Got near beer, soda pop, weak coffee, and strong milk," the man said. Harry indicated the beer taps lining the back of the bar. Without looking, the man added, "Dry as the town you landed in, son."

"Dry?"

"Blame the suffragettes; don't blame me."

"Oh," Harry said. "Well, then, near beer."

"Blaaaah," one of the elderly men grimaced.

His drink came, as did the casual, curious conversation.

"Might be staying around a few days," he added, tipping his beer glass toward the men, "dry or not. Maybe you can recommend a good hotel."

"Well, the Cattleman's clean," one of the men said, "but the food's better at Betty's Boarding House. I know onaccounta when my ol' woman kicked me out last spring, I had to live there. Betty's blueberry buckle can't be beat. Food's so doggone good, in fact, I'm thinking about picking another fight just so she'll kick me out again."

There was laughter from the regulars who knew his wife and Betty.

You'd have to know a man six years before he'd tell you all that on the Bowery, Harry thought with a small, wry smile. "Thanks. I'll check into it."

"You sound like you're from back east," the bartender said. "Boston?"

"New York," Harry said. He pulled the photograph of Hellie out of his pocket. "Don't suppose you've heard a girl around here sounding like me? Here, this girl here." He passed the newspaper photo to the old man closest to him and pointed to Hellie.

The bartender handed him a pair of glasses, and the old man said, "Nope. She don't look familiar. Looks a little like Bess Ackerly's girl, but hell, she's probably pushing fifty years old by now."

"But that other girl," Arnie, the other cowpoke, said, pointing with his cigarette. "*She* looks familiar to me."

It took some rearranging of memory between the two old men, but Arnie finally announced, "Yep. That's it. It was that day you and me was hauled in for tail-tying."

"Tail-tying?" Harry asked, almost dreading what the reply might be.

The bartender leaned over the counter and said, "Meet Ace Quimby and Arnie Meeker, town characters and Oregon's two oldest juvenile delinquents." The old men were laughing as they recalled their perennial practical joke of tying together the tails of horses hitched up in town.

"Yep, we saw them two girls down at the police station! They'd got the collar, too!"

"But not for tail-tying," Ace said, as though that was an important point.

"What for? Do you remember?" Harry asked.

Arnie scratched his chin, which had gone several days without a shave. "Hmm, I think they was shoplifters."

"No, pickpockets!" Ace corrected.

"You sure they weren't hookers?" the bartender asked. "Hattie at the Red Hat was bringing girls in special for Round-Up." Then, to Harry, "Too bad you missed it."

"No, Ed, these was just tykes!" Ace said. "Look at 'em. Besides, you know Captain Barksdale goes easy on hookers near Round-Up time."

"She's supposed to be living on some rich ranch," Harry said.

The men all looked at each other. "Well, we got plenty of those!" the bartender said. That was followed by the locals joking, naming names, and arguing over net worths.

"Hey, sonny," a gruff voice said from the other end of the bar. "I know them girls." There were five ceramic mugs on the table in front of her. "Ed, give this nice stranger a mug of gourmet elixir," she said. "Put it on my tab. And bring me another."

"Wait just a minute . . . ," Ed said.

"Aw, he ain't no revie-nooer, are you, son?" she gushed, patting the bar stool next to her. "Come on down here and talk to Arla." Two mugs were delivered, and Harry knew what the "gourmet elixir" was by the large woman's breath.

She put on a pair of wire-rimmed glasses and looked at the picture, focused, and said, "I know them girls." She downed the contents of her mug with one appreciative gulp. "Yup. Hellie and Lizzie. Oh, I remember the night the sheriff brought 'em out after they got arrested. Fur sure as hell flew that night! So, what are they to you?"

"That one, nothing. But that one there, she's my sister."

"That Hellie girl? Lord, what a trouble-making spitfire! You sure you want to find her?"

"Ma'am, I come all the way from New York. Yes, I want to find her. Where is she?"

Then, she looked at him with a serious frown. "Wait. Ain't you dead?"

Harry smiled as he drank and said, "It was all a big misunderstanding, and I've come to tell her."

"Well, then drink up, son," she said, dismounting the stool with a wobble. She zigzagged down the bar and held out her plump hand. "Ed, my crank."

"You know our arrangement, Arla. You don't get your crank until you pay your tab."

She looked at Harry with as close to a demure smile as she could form in her sloppy state. Harry put money on the counter, and Arla reached for her car's hand crank.

Ed said, "Arla, you passed drunk about an hour ago. You know I'm breaking all the rules with you."

"Yeah, 'specially the rule says women gotta set in back booths and not at the bar with you wild and woolly menfolk," she said, indicating the men who all raised their mugs to her. "But Pendleton ain't much on rules, thank the lord. Besides, this handsome young man here is driving. Ain't you?"

She put on her worn felt hat, cocked it lopsided, while Ed handed the crank to Harry. "Can you city boys crank start a car and drive?" Arla asked.

"Some."

"Well, some is enough to get us where we're going."

"Is it far? I'm beat from the trip."

"Not if you can drive like you say." She wove a little, and Harry helped to steady her and escort her out the door, handing her his valise while he carried the leather case.

Once the Model T finally started and Harry found the gears, he followed Arla's pointing on the road out of Pendleton and toward the moonlit Hidden Hills.

Harry took in the vast, undulating landscape, the impressive ironworks announcing the Hidden Hills, and finally the lush valley that enveloped the grounds, the trees, and the mansion beyond.

He swallowed hard and felt a dryness in his throat. "Wow."

"That's what they all say," Arla said, now holding her forehead with her hand. "Try to miss the bumps, okay, son?"

"Hellie lives *here*?"

"Well, not in the big house. Out back. The washhouse. Here, go right and turn off the lights. Here! Turn." She indicated a road that bypassed the long drive and the immediate detection of Mrs. Gorence. "We'll go out back. Best you and your sis meet up where you two can be alone. And where I can sneak in the house."

Harry drove around to the back and was told to park the Model T in a barn. He helped Arla out. "Where's Hellie?"

"See that building there, with all the steam rising out? That's the washhouse. She's in there, and if she ain't, then she will be shortly. Sure would like to see her face when she sees you." Arla pulled him by the arm. "Now, I won't tell the missus about you if you don't tell no one about me and where you found me."

"Fine."

"And *how* you found me," she added with a grin. "We got a deal?"

"Deal."

"So you *hitched* a ride out here?"

"Sure. Thanks. You okay to walk?"

"Son, I been walking under the effects of some sort of booze or another since before your mama was born," she said, a maternal grin spreading across her face. "Just point me toward that great big white house and these legs'll do the rest."

She lumbered off, her purse slung over her shoulder, her shopping bag swinging at her side. Harry steadied himself against a wave of dizziness and blamed Arla's "gourmet elixir." He dragged the leather case into a corner of the barn, covered it with a tarp, then took his valise and, staying well hidden by moving from tree to post to bush, walked the short distance to the washhouse.

Hellie had seen the stranger out of the corner of her eye. She caught the dude's hat, the dark blue suit, just as the figure dashed behind a bush in the shadowy dusk of the day.

"Damn soap peddlers," she growled. "Sneaking out here at all hours." She grabbed Slim and one of the marbles she kept for ammo. She drew it back and took aim as the door slowly opened.

Harry walked into the fork of the drawn slingshot. "Stop it right there, you cheapjack son-of-a . . ." The low-throated growl of her street voice slowly faded away. The slingshot came down, and they were face to face.

Harry had prepared himself for tears, a leap into his arms, a praise god! a speechless gasp. But he hadn't prepared himself for Hellie shooting him in the toe with Slim.

"Ow!" he hollered, grabbing his toe and hopping on one foot. "What'd you do that for?"

"I knew you wasn't dead! I knew it! So why'd Flip tell me that? Harry! That's for the worst thing you ever did to me!" She grabbed for the marble. "Stand still, I'm gonna shoot the other foot!"

"Hellie! Hellie! Stop it! I got lots to tell you! Hellie, stop! This any way to treat me after all I done to get here?"

He grabbed her shoulders to settle her, and they slowly grinned as they took each other in. Finally, she threw her arms around him. "Harry! You *are* alive! I thought I was shooting a ghost!"

She led him into her back room where the light was better and where they could talk. "There's a lot to tell you, too," she said. "How did you find me . . . how? where . . . ? What'd you do? Walk from New York? You're so sunburned."

Once under the overhead light, Harry did look flushed. "No, I came by train, but I caught a cold traveling out here. Say, it's hot in here, Hellie. How do you stand it?"

"It's amazing what you can get used to once you get used to it," she said, giving him another hard glance. "But how did you find me way out here?"

"You know me—I got ways." She handed him a glass of water, which he downed. "Thanks. Feels good on my throat."

She felt his forehead and said, "You're hot, Harry."

The touch of her cool hand on his forehead reminded him how tired and achy he felt, what a long journey it had been. "Think I could lie down a bit, Hellie? Then we can talk after I have a nap."

Harry shuffled toward the bunks. "Which one can I sleep on?" he asked. But he collapsed on the nearest bunk, leaned his head back, and whispered, "Just a little nap, okay, Hellie?"

He was asleep before she could even respond.

She looked down at his sleeping face. Was it really him? Was Harry really right here before her? Wasn't the Harry she left in New York a street pup in rags? Who was this natty young dandy? His ruddy complexion was accented by the growth of dark stubble around his chin and his hair seemed thicker. Had he grown?

She pulled off his shoes, lifted his heavy legs onto the bed, covered him, and felt his forehead.

He was on fire. She pulled the blanket off him and closed the dampers on the woodstove to put the fire out and cracked a window open.

By ten that evening, she knew she had to get help.

"Oh, lord almighty! Who is that?" Birdy asked, looking down at Harry. Hellie had pulled her awake and brought her to the washhouse. The room smelled of sickness and was chilly after Hellie had cut the heat.

"It's Harry. My brother. He's sick, Birdy. Look at him. What do I do?"

"Oh my god," she said, touching his forehead. "How did he get here?"

"I don't know. He just showed up. All the way from New York," Hellie said, putting a cold, wet cloth on his forehead.

"Mrs. G. is going to have to know about this," Birdy stated.

"She'll turn him away. I know she will. He's come to take me home."

"Well, he isn't taking anyone anywhere right now."

"Birdy, I think it's that flu everyone is talking about."

"Now, it could be a hundred different things. Did he say anything before he took sick? Has he been around anyone sick?"

"Swear to God, Birdy, he just walked in here a few hours ago! Right out of thin air! He said he was tired and wanted to sleep. But he's not waking up."

Birdy pursed her lips, looking down at Harry. "Close those windows and start up that fire again," she ordered. "After that, start up the washing machines—every one of them, to get some moisture in here."

"What for? Birdy, don't we have to cool him down?" Hellie said.

"No, we have to break his fever," she said. "We'll make a sweat lodge. That's how my grandfather cured just about every ailment in my village when I was a girl."

Harry coughed so deep that it resonated throughout the room. Both Birdy and Hellie looked down at him. "Get pillows! Prop him up," Birdy ordered.

Harry objected, but they got him almost into a sitting position, and his breathing came easier.

"It's hot," he said, eyes fluttering. "Geez, it's hot. Let's take a swim, Hellie. Want to head down to Coney?"

Birdy said, "That's the fever talking, Hellie. Don't let it bother you too much. Just do like I say. We have to keep him drinking water and we need a thermometer."

"Are you going to tell Mrs. G.?" Hellie asked.

"No, you are," Birdy replied, looking past Hellie.

Standing in the doorway was Mrs. Gorence, with Lizzie behind her, peering into the washhouse.

"What the hell is going on here?" she demanded. She wore an old lamb fleece jacket so large and crusty it could have stood in a corner on its own.

"It's my brother," Hellie said. "Come to find me."

"I thought he was dead," Mrs. Gorence said, staring coldly at her.

Harry coughed again. "Me too," said Hellie. "He's sick, ma'am. Real bad."

Lizzie put her hand to her mouth, and Mrs. Gorence said, "Lizzie, you go to the house and don't you dare come back out here. Wash your hands before you tend to Joey. Do you understand?"

"Hellie," Lizzie said. "Is it really Harry? How . . ."

"Dammit, girl! Do as I say!"

Mrs. Gorence turned her stony gaze on Hellie. "How dare you bring sickness out here?"

"I didn't. He just showed up on my doorstep. Swear to God. I don't know how he even knew I was in Pendleton, let alone at the Hills. What was I supposed to do?"

Mrs. Gorence looked at Harry, then back to Hellie. She took a deep breath, then said, "Go to Arla's window and wake her up. Tell her to call Doctor Cornell. But do not go inside, understand?"

Perhaps it was the dim light and the eerie shadows it cast on Mrs. Gorence, but was that the trace of a smile? Not her famous sarcastic, get-even type of smile, but a small, almost tender and understanding smile?

"Are you going to just stand there staring at me or are you going to do as I say?" The woman's voice was as formidable as always. Hellie snapped out of it, pulled a blanket around her shoulders, and headed for the door.

"Birdy," Mrs. Gorence said, letting the ancient fleece coat slip off. "What can I do?"

Doctor Cornell put his stethoscope back in his bag and said, "Hard to tell, Scholastica. His lungs sound pretty thick. Especially on this side." He looked at Hellie and said, "You know anything about this scar? It's very recent."

"He got shot," she said, with a cautious glance toward Mrs. Gorence. "You think that made him sick?"

"This is a surgical scar. It doesn't look too close to his lung, but he definitely has an infection. Don't want this to turn into pneumonia."

"He thought it was just a bad cold," Hellie said.

"Has he been around anyone else who's been sick?" the doctor asked.

"I don't know," Hellie said. "He's been talking crazy."

"Is it influenza, Doctor?" Mrs. Gorence asked. Hellie noticed an uncharacteristic tinge of uncertainty in her voice.

"Hard to say. I'm no big-city doc, but I don't think you have much to worry about. Personally, I think there's too much panic over this Spanish flu. Every year some sort of flu takes hold and the newspapers can't wait to tally the dead. Where did you say he came from?"

"New York," Hellie said.

Mrs. Gorence and Dr. Cornell caught each other's eyes. "Well, they certainly have had flu cases back east. Boston and Philadelphia. Army camps and such. Did your brother just return from the war?"

"I don't know where he's been for the last five months. I thought he was dead. Of that," and she pointed to his gunshot wound.

"Well, let's just see how it goes. Fever of one hundred and three isn't death's doorstep. Granted, it's no fun. And Birdy, no more of your shaman sweat lodge. That's nothing but witch-doctoring. Cool him down. And here, give him these," the doctor said, handing Hellie a small green bottle. "Aspirin. It'll bring down his fever. Stop the pain. He's young. I'm sure he'll be just fine in a couple of days. Two aspirin every four hours should bring his fever down. Crush it up if he can't swallow pills. But for God's sake, cool him down. Let me know if that cough gets worse."

Mrs. Gorence showed him out and returned. Hellie opened the bottle of pills, smelled them, then dashed two out on her hand.

"No," Birdy said, placing her hand on Hellie's. "Don't give him those. Fever kills the sickness, so why would we want to kill the fever?"

Hellie looked at Mrs. Gorence, for the first time ever, for instruction. "Go against the doctor?" she asked.

"He's your brother," Mrs. Gorence said. "Your decision."

"These pills are new," Birdy said. "Sweat lodges have been curing my people for generations."

The heat, the stench of vomit, and the horror of seeing her brother so sick and helpless made Hellie want to scream and run away as far as her legs would carry her. Off into the frosty night. A train to anywhere but here. Of all the times she'd wished she and Harry could be together again, taking on all comers, why, why did this have to happen? She was better off thinking he was dead. What's the purpose of getting her brother back only to watch him writhe in a fever, maybe even die?

"I . . . I . . . ," she said, looking down at Harry. "I can't think."

"Hellie, we take care of our own out here," Mrs. Gorence said, giving her a confident nod.

"Okay, your way first," she said to Birdy, recapping the bottle. "Then these if all else fails."

Mrs. Gorence said, "Birdy, stoke the fire. Hellie, fill pots with water and put them on the stove."

Within an hour the three had changed Hellie's living quarters into a makeshift sweat lodge. Birdy had nailed blankets to block the chill of the two windows and to keep it dark once daylight came. Hellie strung lines in the rafters so sheets could be hung down, keeping Harry's bunk isolated.

Hellie systematically went through the entire washhouse, wiping down with bleach anything Harry could have possibly touched. The woodburning stove was stoked to a roar, and the two water-filled pots on top rolled a steady steam into the room. The three washing machines were kept running, adding to the growing, steamy heat, making the washhouse feel like a Swedish sauna.

Hellie, Mrs. Gorence, and Birdy worked in their underclothes to keep themselves cool. Their faces were flushed, sweat ran shamelessly, wet hair curled around faces. They took turns standing outside in the cool night air and guzzling water.

Hellie noticed how Mrs. Gorence was moving slower and slower, her limp more pronounced. "You don't have to stay out here, Mrs. G. I can do all this. You go back to the house and get some rest. You too, Birdy. He's my brother and I'll . . ."

The women exchanged knowing glances. Again, that slight smile on Mrs. Gorence's small, sweat-beaded face. "No, Hellie. We all have to stay here now."

"Why?"

"In case this is that flu . . ." She looked at Birdy and added, "We can't take a chance on spreading it." Mrs. Gorence sat on a bench next to the washing machines and rubbed her bad leg.

"The doc didn't think it was, though. He didn't think it was anything to worry about. And Harry's sleeping better."

"Doctor Cornell's a good man, but he's been wrong before," Mrs. Gorence said.

Harry started coughing in the back room, and Hellie went to him. She changed the cloth on his forehead and gently wiped the sweat from his face.

His eyes fluttered open and slowly focused on Hellie, but he wasn't able to speak for the coughing spasm. Hellie cleaned the blood-tinged spit from his lips.

"Damn you, Harry," she whispered. "Damn you all to hell."

"Don't come any closer, Lizzie," Hellie said, standing on the porch to the washhouse.

"Hellie, what's happening out there?" Lizzie asked, wrapping her shawl around her against the chill of the October dawn.

"We have to stay here and none of you can come near us. Mrs. G.'s orders. We need some food, though. And coffee. Mrs. G. says to gather all the carbolic soap and alcohol you can find and bring it over. Wake Perry and tell him what's happening. He's gotta tell the hands to stay away."

"But what about you?" Lizzie asked.

Until that moment, it hadn't occurred to Hellie that she was in any danger of catching it. Or Birdy. Or Mrs. G. "Too late to think about that now."

Hellie said she would use her slingshot to ping pebbles against the kitchen windows if she needed anything. "Oh, we need some toilet paper for our outhouse. And ask Arla to start up some chicken broth. Don't spare the salt. When Harry comes out of it, he'll be hungry. And sandwiches for us."

"You mean when Arla comes out of it. She sure has a hangover. Stumbling around like a zombie."

Just as Harry and the Pope had their clandestine drops, so Hellie and Lizzie had theirs. The stump that held a birdbath in the summer was now the halfway mark where food and articles were left by Lizzie and then picked up by Hellie.

"Guess what?" Lizzie said to Hellie as she stepped away from the stump with the noontime meal.

"What?"

"Joey took a step."

"No! Using that special shoe Perry made up?"

"You should have seen his face! I don't know who was more surprised—him or me!"

"Wish I could have seen that. Wish *she* could have."

"What's it like, in such close quarters with . . ." Even outside with no one around, she whispered, " . . . the witch?"

"She's been pretty quiet. I don't know, sort of, well, different, Lizzie. She's still shouting orders, but you know, I kind of think she'd be in there helping me even if she wasn't stuck there. You know?"

"And your brother?"

"I don't know, Lizzie . . . I think he's . . ."

"Hellie!" Mrs. Gorence shouted from the porch. "Stop your yapping and bring that food in while it's still hot!"

"*Hot* food. Just what we need in that sweatbox. See you," Hellie said, taking the heavy tray off the stump.

"I wish there was something more I could do to help," Lizzie said.

"I'd kill for some iced tea," Hellie said.

"I'll make some. Hey, don't you get sick, okay?"

"Okay."

Hellie startled awake from her dozing and went to Birdy, who was standing with a hanging sheet draped over her shoulder, looking down at Harry.

"How is he?" she asked.

"No better, no worse," Birdy replied, letting the sheet fall back.

Hellie looked at Mrs. Gorence, sleeping in a small lump on a damp mattress on the washroom floor, oblivious to the now steady drone of the machines and the boiler that seemed to groan for someone to come to their senses and turn it off.

Hellie knelt next to the old woman and gently fanned her sweat-beaded, flushed face. "You can't keep this up," she whispered down to her.

But she did keep it up. Birdy and Mrs. Gorence both worked in tireless shifts, ministered to Harry as though he was their own flesh and blood.

And so it went for the next two days. They kept the fires roaring, the air warm and moist, until Harry's fever broke and his delirium subsided. On the third day Harry was finally, finally sitting up, weak as a newborn lamb, but sipping broth between dry coughing fits. He'd conquered what they now knew must surely be the dreaded Spanish influenza.

On the fourth day, Hellie felt a soreness deep in her throat.

48

Harry continued to recover, moved now to one of the mattresses next to the washing machines, sleeping in fourteen-hour blocks solid, still too weak to converse much or see to his own personal needs. His cough was still constant, but it was dry and clear and free of pneumonia. His cheeks were still pale, his eyes sunken.

Mrs. Gorence and Birdy hauled his sweat-soaked mattress and bed clothes outside, where they were piled and ordered burned.

"Where's Hellie?" he whispered, taking a glass of water with a shaky hand.

"In there. Sick," Birdy said. "You'd think one of us old ladies would have been next. But Hellie's sick now."

"Aw," he whispered. "Hellie's too mean to stay sick long."

"Hellie's a lot of things, but mean isn't one of them," Birdy said.

"You got to get her well. She and me got plans." He lay back down and put his arm over his stinging, bloodshot eyes.

"The only plan for you is to stay put. Get some strength back," Birdy said, putting his ice water down next to him.

He dozed off, waking several hours later when he felt the overwhelming presence of a large figure standing between him and the window light.

He looked up, his eyes still aching. "Who are you?" he asked.

"Don't you remember me, sonny?" she growled, in a heavy, hoarse whisper.

He squinted and said, "Oh, the woman with the gourmet elixir," he said. "I think it was poison."

"No! *You* got *me* sick!" she said. She looked down at him, then buckled at the knees and fell to the floor in a tremendous heap.

Mrs. Gorence and Birdy ran into the room. "Oh, my god! It's Arla!" Birdy said, rushing to her. She felt her forehead. "Burning up." She knelt and brought the cook's heavy head onto her lap. "Arla! Arla," she said.

Mrs. Gorence froze in the doorway to the back room, steadying herself in the threshold. "Arla? How? How? She hasn't come close to us. How?"

Harry brought himself up on an elbow. "I know how," he said. "That's the woman I came out here with."

"Why didn't you tell us that before?" Mrs. Gorence demanded. "Why didn't you say you and her . . . ?"

"We had a deal to clam up about that," Harry said.

Birdy and Mrs. Gorence managed the large, semiconscious woman to a bunk. While the women tended to Arla, Harry came into the makeshift ward and gently pulled back the sheet curtain around Hellie's little bunk.

"Hey," he said. "Looks like the tables are turned, huh? Me looking down and you looking up."

She smiled weakly and coughed. "Arla too?" she asked.

"Aw, she'll be fine. Just pour some booze down her throat," he said. Hellie laughed a little. "You get well fast," he said to her. "I got plans for us, Hellie."

"Like what?" she asked.

"You ain't in no shape to hear 'em, and I'm still a little shaky."

Harry looked at the wall above Hellie's bunk. Tacked there were the familiar dog-eared photographs of their mother and the war poster Hellie had stolen—the mother and child, drifting down deep into an emerald sea.

He closed the curtain and returned to his mattress, where he fell into a sound, exhausted sleep.

When he awoke again, it was to the sound of gentle pebbles dashing on the window over his mattress. He looked up, ran his hand across to remove the steam, and saw a girl standing several yards away. He opened the window. "You that friend of Hellie's? Tizzie? Missy?" he said, his voice slow to return.

"Lizzie," she said, feeling her side lock to make sure it was adequately covering her face. "Where's Hellie? She hasn't come to pick up breakfast." She indicated the tree stump with the linen-covered tray still on top. "She okay?"

"She took sick."

Lizzie's face froze. "Oh, no. And now Arla, too?"

"It's pretty catching," Harry said. "But I pulled out okay. Hellie's strong."

"I hope you're right. I need to talk to Mrs. G. Can you bring her to the window for me?"

Harry called to her.

"Lizzie, what is it?" Mrs. G. asked, an urgent snap to her voice.

"It's okay, Mrs. G., Joey's fine. He's upstairs napping."

"How close of contact has Joey had with Arla the last few days?"

"Not much. You know Joey still doesn't take much to her."

"Have you cleaned everything just like I told you? I mean everything? Even things you don't think anyone's touched for years? Nothing goes in that child's mouth that hasn't been sterilized first."

"No, nothing."

"And Perry's been staying well away? All the hands are staying clear of the house? No one to or from town?"

"Yes, ma'am."

"Good." Then, as an abrupt afterthought, "And you?"

"Fine," she said. "I never get sick. Mrs. G., Doctor Cornell called. He said there's three cases of the flu in town. Ace Quimby just passed. He said you'd know him. He has to make a report to the health department. He wants to know how many cases we have and to bring the new cases to the hospital in town."

"Call him back and tell him thanks, but we're taking care of our own just fine. Tell him three cases." She paused, then added, "With God's mercy, *just* three cases."

Lizzie indicated the tray. "The tray's heavy. You want me to bring it over to you?"

"No! Just leave it sit. Birdy will get it as soon as she's done with Arla. Oh, Lizzie?" Mrs. Gorence called. Lizzie turned. "Now get that damn end-of-the-world look off your face. This isn't the worst thing that's ever hit the Hidden Hills. We're going to be just fine."

Lizzie offered a small smile. "Okay," she said.

"You don't believe me, do you?" she said, in her usual commanding manner.

"Well, you got her brother recovered."

"As I will the others," she said, closing the window.

Hellie had every right to think she was dying. The flu took her in its grip, invaded every cell in her body, and clutched her as a mother clutches her dying baby. *Dying baby, dying baby,* Hellie's fevered thoughts ran. She saw the war poster of the drowned mother and child, the icy waters taking them down, down, down forever. Hellie longed for those icy waters running over her body, as the heat of the room, the fever in her body, the boiling steam all seemed to rise and play among the rafters, only to evaporate and rain back down on her in the form of singeing droplets of fire.

Fire . . . fire . . . fire . . . , she thought. *Get used to it, Hellie Jondoe.*

In and out of consciousness, in and out of fits of coughing, in and out of life itself, Hellie knew that Arla, just a sheet away from her, was doing far worse. The depth of her coughs, the timbre of her moans, the whispers of Birdy and Mrs. Gorence. She knew Arla would beat her to death's doorstep. *Good,* she thought. *I'll have a friend waiting for me in hell . . .*

"No," she thought she heard Mrs. Gorence say, low but firm. "I'll give you last rites, if you insist, but you're not going to die, so stop talking about it."

Me? Hellie wondered. *Is she talking to me?*

"But I ain't been baptized. I want a man of the cloth."

Did I just say that? No, that's not my voice. That's Arla. Good ol' Arla.

"Piffle! Here," Mrs. Gorence said. "I baptize you in the name of the father, the mother, and the holy ghost."

"The *son*," Birdy corrected. "The father, the *son*, and the holy ghost."

Hellie smiled to envision the expression on Mrs. G.'s face—probably annoyed and only a little apologetic. "Oh, of course. Go ahead, Birdy. You say it. That way, she's covered no matter what. And use that gin."

"That's what I like about you, old woman," Arla said, in and out of weak gasps. "Always looking out for the help. And put the gin on my lips, not my forehead, Birdy."

Hellie wished she had the strength to pull back the sheet and watch the three women, old friends somehow, after all. Birdy and Mrs. G. standing over the huge bulk of Arla. Bickering, laughing, ordering, drinking gin—maybe even holding each other's hands as friends are supposed to do when one is passing.

What would they say, do, when it was her time, for surely no one can live through this ache, this fever, this fear, this flu except one as immortal as *Harry. Harry. Harry.* Hellie wasn't sure if she was dreaming she was calling his name or if she really was. *Harry, Harry, Harry.* It didn't matter, because he wasn't coming to her in any form. Then she began to wonder if everything, his return, his sickness, her own sickness, was maybe some horrible nightmare and soon, soon, please God soon, she would awaken.

She had no idea what day it was, let alone what time. Her head was now on the opposite end of the bunk, her sheets having been changed several times. Vague recollections came back, but only as fuzzy, blurry images. Bedpan, puke bucket, coughing into paper, the squeak of the heavy iron stove door as it opened, closed, opened, closed. *God, these blankets are heavy.* And water, always water being thrust to her lips.

The room now was calm and quiet. She heard someone in the outer room. "Birdy? Harry?" she called, voiceless, then in a hoarse whisper. "Who's there?"

The sheet was swept aside and Birdy appeared. "Well, that's the first I've been able to understand you for two days, Hellie." She felt her forehead. "Still hot, but not as bad. How do you feel?"

"Like Matthew, Mark, Luke, and Lucifer all hauled a load of coal over me. Twice," she said, falling back down into the mountain of pillows.

"You're talking delirious again," Birdy said.

"Can't I lie down flat? My afterpiece is killing me."

"No, you keep elevated," Birdy said. "Keeps your lungs clearer." She took Hellie's wrist and squeezed it to feel for the rate and strength of her pulse.

"My heart beating?"

"You're not dead yet. Drink some water."

"I'm going to float away," Hellie said, taking another sip of water. "Where is everyone? It's so quiet."

"We moved your brother to a guest room in the main house. He's fine. Damn weak, though. Had a bit of a setback. Lizzie will take care of him."

"Lizzie's got enough to keep her busy," Hellie said. "Harry should be taking care of himself by now. What about Arla? She sleeping?"

"Arla passed two days ago," Birdy said, laying Hellie's wrist back on her chest.

"But she was so big and strong," Hellie said.

"I know," she said. "She went downhill so fast, no one, not God, not plain old good luck could have saved her. It was her time. I'm sure going to miss her."

"Where is she? I mean . . ."

"Buried her on a hill way out back."

Hellie looked at her and whispered, "Yeah, I think I know it. Where's Mrs. G. right now? Quarantine over?"

"She's sleeping," Birdy said, indicating the washroom. "No, she and I are staying here a few more days. Just to make sure."

"She okay?" Hellie asked.

"Don't know where she gets her strength," Birdy said. "You had a bad thirty-six hours. Mrs. G. didn't leave you once. I'm going to let her sleep. Don't know how she could ever fight this off, if she gets it."

"Thirty-six hours?"

"Yep, and her with a bad leg. Now, enough talking. You sleep."

Hellie put her head back down and whispered, "If Harry hadn't come out here, Arla'd still be alive."

"How do you figure?"

"Well, he had to have been the one brought us the flu, don't you think?"

"I think you'll drive yourself crazy if you start thinking about that," Birdy said. "Well, young lady, I think the window can be opened now, just a crack."

"Cool air?" Hellie asked. "No more sweat lodge?"

"Well, we're going to keep it warm in here, but I think your fever has broken. You have a long way to go, Hellie, so just get some more sleep."

"You okay, Birdy? Lizzie, Joey, Perry, the hands?

"Yes, so far, so good. Mrs. G. said no one could go to Pendleton or come near here. We've been totally isolated. Wish more folks would just stay put till this epidemic is over."

"How come she knows the right thing to do?" Hellie asked, feeling her eyelids grow heavy.

"Ask her. She might tell you someday."

Exactly two weeks had passed since Harry arrived at the Hidden Hills.

When Hellie awoke that morning in late October, it was to a bright fall sun shining through the window. Her sheets were dry and crisp and, for once, didn't smell of sickness or sweat but of bleach and fresh air. The sheet partition was swept aside, and there stood Lizzie, holding the chubby hands of Joey, standing between Lizzie's legs.

"Look who's come to show off his two working legs," Lizzie said.

"It's okay for you to be here?" Hellie said, sitting up.

"Yep. Flu's gone. Doctor said we all got by pretty good. Said there's just a few folks in town getting over it. All in all, thirty-nine cases and only six deaths."

That brought an image of Arla's huge smile to Hellie's mind. "Only . . . poor Arla. She sure went fast. Did you go to her burial?"

"No, Mrs. G. made me stay in the house with Joey all this time. This is about the first time we've even been farther than the birdbath. I never thought I'd say I miss this place, but that big house is lonely when it's only me and Joey."

"Come here, you little rascal!" Hellie said, reaching over and pulling Joey up onto her bunk. "Did you miss me, buddy? Miss ol' Hellie?"

He objected and wanted down. "Now that he can walk, he doesn't want to be held," said Lizzie. "It's practically killing Birdy."

"Hey, where's Harry?" Hellie said. "He hasn't been around in a few days. He still okay?"

"Hellie, you sure you two aren't Catholic?"

"I'd remember being Catholic. Why?"

"Well, I overheard Harry talking long distance on the telephone last night. Real late. Joey's working on a tooth, so I was up with him and I heard Harry. I could swear he said 'I have to talk to the pope.'"

"You're hearing things. If he's gone Catholic, I've grown a third leg. And besides, no one just telephones the pope. Do they?"

"No, I guess not. Gosh, Mrs. G. is going to be livid when she sees that phone bill, huh? It probably costs a million dollars to call the pope, no matter who he is."

"He probably said 'dope,' not 'pope.' He's got that street way of talking, you know."

"Well, he did talk strange. He said he was writing to say he got work. Real good work."

"Work? Harry?" Hellie said. "You must have been half asleep, Lizzie. Harry doesn't *work*."

Lizzie's face turned serious. "Hellie, Mrs. G. asked Harry what his intentions were this morning, and he said he was taking you away."

Hellie paused, then, "And what did she say?"

"Birdy caught me eavesdropping from the kitchen and sent me out here."

Hellie placed Joey on the floor and stood up. "Careful, now, Hellie," Lizzie warned. "You got to get steady on your feet."

"No, I'm going over there. No one's talking about Hellie Jondoe without her having a say! Not anymore! Not Mrs. G. and not Harry!"

"Somebody call my name?" Harry said, appearing at the door. "Hellie, what're you doing up? Alls I need is you taking sick again."

"Harry, what were you and Mrs. G. talking about?"

Lizzie and Joey scooted outside, leaving brother and sister alone.

Harry and Hellie sat at the table in Hellie's quarters. "What were you and Mrs. G. talking about this morning?" she asked again.

"You."

"What about me?"

"I told her I'm your brother and I got every right in the world to take you back home."

"She agreed?"

"After we talked some, yes."

"Just like that? Said I could go?" Hellie asked.

"Said I could drive Arla's Model T and leave it in town. Said there's a train heading east tomorrow at noon."

"Just like that? Nothing about needing me or . . ."

"You know me," Harry said, grinning. "I got ways with women. Even dried-up old crones." He smiled, then looked around the room. "So, where you keeping it?"

"What?"

"Your stash." He walked to a cupboard under a bunk and pulled it open.

"What stash?"

Harry stopped and looked at her. "Don't tell me you're holding out on your own brother."

Hellie stared at him, wondering if the fever had maybe melted her memory. Then, "Harry, I don't have anything to hold out. I'm flat broke."

Harry sat back down, grinning. "Sure you are. Hell, just what I've seen in silver over in that house could finance the war. You can't tell me you haven't been putting something away for a rainy day."

She leaned back in her chair as though to get a clearer look at Harry, thinking before answering. Finally, "Yeah. I guess you *would* think I've been lifting off that old lady."

"Sure, just like I taught you. Remember? Pick out the weak ones in the crowd? Take a little slice now and then and no one's the wiser."

"That's what you taught me, all right."

"Look, Hellie. It don't matter, 'cause I got it all fixed up for us. After you left New York, well, I got me a new angle. A new game."

"What?" she asked. Suddenly, the streets of the Bowery and angles and games were a lifetime away.

"Just a sweet little racket. Got me a new partner, too. No more penny-ante stuff for us, Hellie. Wait till you see the apartment we're getting. And I like driving cars and think I'll get us one. You, well, there's this new girls' school opening up in Manhattan and . . ."

"Stop it, Harry! What racket?"

"I'm in pharama—pharama, what'd the Pope call it?"

"Pope?" Hellie asked.

"Yeah, my new partner. Pharmaceuticals! That's what we're in."

"What're they?"

He leaned closer to her, cast her a charming, worldly smile, and whispered, "Drugs. And it's pure pudding. Easiest grift in the world."

"You mean like heroin? You're a dope peddler? Thought you said that was a dead man's racket."

"Oh, the Pope and me, we got plans, Hellie," he went on. "We're going to get a piece of the rum-running racket, too. This Prohibition bit is here to stay. Get in on the ground floor. That's what them Wall Street tycoons say."

"Drugs and booze?" Hellie said.

Harry returned her gaze with cool confidence. "I know what I'm doing, Hellie. Your job ain't to question what I do."

"Just what is my job?"

"To come back with me, get some schooling. Become a lady. When we're setting high, you got to, you know, be the lady of the house. Till I get me a wife, then you're out on your bum," he added, giving her a playful shove.

But Hellie didn't laugh. "What if I don't want to do any of that? What if I want to stay me? Just Hellie?"

"Don't be stupid, Hellie. All girls want that high society bit. You'll love our new life. Wait and see."

Hellie watched Harry's handsome face. She nodded her head slowly, thinking as Harry went on. "So, you just pack your things and don't bother with the rags, Hellie. We'll stop over in Chicago and buy you some real ladies' clothes. Now that I got the dough, I can get you good stuff."

"So, is Flip in on your new enterprise?"

Harry's face darkened. "The little spider got hisself killed. Wasn't even in the line of duty. C. K. and his new troops got him. But I got him the best damn funeral money could buy, Hellie. I did right by ol' Flip. And don't worry. I ain't done with C. K. I'll corner him soon as we're back in New York. I'll get even. Don't you worry."

Hellie felt weak and woozy, but she was certain it wasn't from the effects of the flu.

"Oh! That reminds me!" Harry said, jumping up. "You stay right here. This flu sure does make your head all funny! I'm forgetting everything!"

Hellie watched him dash out and toward the barn next to the smokehouse.

When he reappeared he was toting the large leather case that Amanda Collier had pressed into his keeping.

51

"Amanda's dead, too?" Hellie asked.

"You know," Harry said, a spark of enlightenment coming to his face. "I'll bet that's where I caught the flu! From her! Why, sure. She must have been at the catching stage when I saw her about your photograph." He looked at Hellie, who was looking at the envelope addressed "Miss Hellie Jondoe." "You want me to read that for you?" Harry asked, reaching for it.

"I can read some now, Harry," Hellie said, sitting and carefully slitting the envelope open. "Just hand me my glasses." She put them on and said, "You laugh at me, I'll get Slim." Then, sounding out each syllable, she read the first letter she had ever received.

My dear Hellie,

It's hard to imagine where you are right now and what you have been doing, who you are with, what sort of young woman you are becoming. I see only the very best, you may sure.

As your brother has been the one to present this to you, you know that I have passed from this earth. The dead are living and the living are dead. What a world, wouldn't you agree? You were very much on my mind during the end, as the enclosed will attest.

Hellie looked at Harry and asked, "What's attest?"

"You know, a test is what they give you in school to see how dumb you are."

"I don't think that's what she means."

"Well, what's she say? What else is in that big envelope? Money?"

Hellie, her brow lined, returned to the letter:

> I have sent you some photography equipment. Nothing fancy, just some basics. I remember your sense of wonder about a face being "froze up in time." Anyone who feels that will be a fine photographer some day. The books will teach you how. But the best teacher is to just start taking photographs yourself. Photograph everything! Also in this envelope is a contract from a very important newspaper. Get someone who knows about such things to explain it to you. What I want you to do is write the story of your journey west. Your own words are best. And photographs, Hellie! Take photographs. Then mail them to the address on the contract. I have also written to these people to expect to hear from you.
>
> My dear Hellie, I grow weary and I have already pressed upon my nurse enough of my last correspondences. Grow well, Hellie. Learn to see the world through your own lens. And once in a while, think about me, your friend,
>
> Amanda Beulah Emmaline Collier
> *Photographer-Journalist*

Hellie set the letter down. Harry said, "Well? Took you long enough, Hellie. It wasn't no book, just a letter."

"There were big words," Hellie said.

"I know them," he said, reaching for the letter.

Hellie snatched it away. "No, it's private. It's my letter, Harry."

She pulled out a camera and looked at him through the lens. The camera slowly came down, and she said, "I only knew her a short time. And she left me all this."

"The Red Cross nurse said she didn't have no kin," Harry said, toying with the folding leg of the tripod.

"*Any* kin," she corrected. "No, she was an orphan herself. Got adopted out on an orphan train, too."

"Well, all that's behind you now, Hellie. I'm taking you away from this daisyville. Get you away from all these cow-hicks. Got you working as a washerwoman and seeing after some little crawler, for Christ's sake. I got some making up to do, don't I?" He picked up the camera and added, "Say, I wonder what we can pawn all this for."

Hellie took it back and said, "No. I'm keeping this."

"Suit yourself. But I ain't hauling that case all the way back to New York after hauling it all the way out here."

Hellie felt oddly chilled and put a log in the stove.

"Aw, come on, Hellie, no more heat! You and me've had enough heat to last us a lifetime. Hell won't be no strange place to us, will it, Hellie?"

"Guess not."

"Not that I'm worried," Harry went on with a swagger. "The bullet didn't kill me. The flu didn't kill me. Think I'll live forever. Well, you do your packing now, Hellie. We're leaving in the morning."

It was the first time Hellie and Lizzie had been invited to dine in the magnificent dining room so heavily laden with the silver they had polished weekly since arriving at the Hidden Hills. Lizzie helped prepare the meal, still trying to figure out Arla's odd cupboard system. Hellie wasn't allowed to stay on her feet for too long a time, so she sat at the worktable in the kitchen and frosted cupcakes for dessert.

"I can't believe you're leaving," Lizzie said, blinking away a tear while she chopped vegetables. "After all we've been through together."

"Well, after all Harry went through to find me, then us getting sick and all. He thinks it's an omen. You know, a sign that we're supposed to stay together. Besides, I caused enough damage around here."

"What's *she* have to say about it?" Lizzie asked, looking toward the ceiling.

"Harry said it's all set. She didn't make no kick. She probably thinks I'm a curse here now."

"Oh, I thought maybe because she's taken to her bed," Lizzie said. "That maybe she's . . ."

"Worrying about her precious laundry," Hellie finished for her.

Birdy entered the kitchen and put a soggy poultice into the sink. "Doctor Cornell just left," she said. "Says it's getting worse." She opened the oven and inspected the roast beef. "Lizzie, you go dress Joey for dinner. I'm turning this oven down. We're having roast beef, not jerky."

"What's getting worse?" Hellie asked, licking some frosting off her fingertip.

Birdy said, "Her polio-myelitis, of course."

"Her what?" Hellie asked.

"It's a disease of the nervous system. It causes paralysis. Don't tell me you haven't noticed her leg."

"You mean all this time she's been sick?" Hellie asked.

"No, she *had* the disease when she was a young woman and every so often the symptoms come back. During times of, oh, stress and over-exertion. That's why she takes to her bed from time to time. Lizzie, take the high chair to the dining room on your way."

When Lizzie had left, Birdy looked at Hellie and said, "It isn't because she's prostrate with grief."

"No, I don't reckon so," Hellie said. "That woman wouldn't know grief if it up and bit her in the butt."

At that, Birdy indicated for Hellie to follow her. They went toward the silver room. "Not more silver to polish!" Hellie said.

Birdy unlocked the room with Arla's key, motioned for Hellie to come inside, then closed the door. Without saying anything, she took out a stool and reached high onto the top shelf. She brought down a large, burgundy-colored silver bag and placed it on the worktable. "Go ahead. Open it," she said.

Hellie pulled open the drawstring and reached inside. She pulled out five heavy silver frames, tarnished black with years of neglect. Each frame held a photograph and had a scrolled engraving below.

"Martin, William, John, Bryant, Theodore," she whispered, looking at the photographs of young, smiling, happy children. She had faces now to match the names on the gravestones. "Her babies."

"There's another frame in there," Birdy said. "Pull that last big one out."

It was a photograph of a handsome man in a military uniform. There was nothing engraved. "Mr. Gorence?"

"Captain Thaddeus Baxter Gorence," Birdy said. "Died in the Spanish-American War. Twenty years gone now."

"Died and left her with all those sons?"

Birdy smiled wistfully as she reached for the frames and, one by one, put them back. "No. Children all died first. That's why the captain left, they say. He left to get away from all the grieving here. Mrs. G. fired everyone—the whole crew, right down to the wranglers. Everyone. Except me. I'm the only one who knows."

"Why? Why'd she fire everyone?" Hellie asked.

"Well, everyone in the territory's got an opinion about that. Mine is she didn't want anyone around her who ever knew the little ones. Then no one could talk and, well, remember. After that, the Hills fell into such a bad state, it's taken us a dozen years to bring it all back. But it's not going to bring those babies back. Or the Captain. They're all dead and buried."

"What killed them? Was it . . . murder?"

"That's what Mrs. G. calls it. It was the diphtheria epidemic of 1894. Mrs. G, being sickly anyway, was first to catch it. Then the baby. Then the others. One by one. Only she survived. She thinks she murdered her babies just as surely as if she took a gun to them."

Hellie couldn't swallow. Five children, a husband . . . total grief, total desertion, all held prisoner by total guilt.

"Well," Birdy continued, "I didn't want you leaving the Hills without knowing. Now you might understand why she is the way she is. Maybe understand why I had such hopes for you and Lizzie here. And Joey. I didn't think she'd ever look at a baby again. Let alone . . . Well, I have to see to dinner."

"Yes," Hellie whispered, envisioning the time when the graves out back were new; a small, broken woman casting seeds . . . vines, briars, brambles springing from the fresh-turned earth to hide the agony and encase the memory.

53

Mrs. Gorence didn't come down for the going-away dinner. Lizzie appeared in the doorway of the dining room holding her untouched dinner tray.

"She didn't want it. Said she wasn't hungry."

"Well, put it down and come take your seat," Birdy said.

Lizzie set the tray on the sideboard and added, "Said she doesn't want to see anyone, to leave her alone and for us to keep it quiet down here." Hellie read Lizzie's lips as she mouthed a silent "*witch*."

It felt odd, almost uncomfortable, sitting at the table, Birdy and Perry across from each other, Joey in his high chair, Harry attacking the food as though it was his last meal for a week, and Lizzie dabbing at her potatoes.

"Well, this isn't much of a party," Birdy finally said. "Perry, go to the kitchen, will you, and in the high cupboard over the icebox is some wine. Will you bring a bottle? I think what we need is just a touch of wine. Just for tonight."

Lizzie and Hellie exchanged glances, remembering the champagne they had stolen from that same cupboard several weeks ago. Perry came back in carrying two bottles and an opener.

"Didn't know if we should have white or red, so I brought both." He laughed a little as he set them down and added, "That ol' Arla! Gone now these two weeks and still having a laugh on us." He held a piece of paper. "It says, 'Deduct from my pay, one bottle of French champagne,' only she sure wasn't much of a speller, was she?"

He handed the note to Birdy, who chuckled and handed it to Hellie, who recognized it as her own labored cursive. "No, she wasn't," Hellie said, handing the note to Lizzie with a tattletale kick under the table.

That started some small talk and the wine did help, but as Birdy had said, it really wasn't much of a going-away party. Lizzie looked like she could cry at any moment, Joey delivered more food to the sheet under his high chair than his mouth, Birdy ate in silence, and Harry lied his way through every polite question Perry asked.

Hellie longed for the solitude of the washhouse, where she could just fall asleep one last time to the steady purr of the boiler, wake up, wash up, and get the Hellie out of the Hidden Hills. How many nights had she planned just such an escape?

"The train leaves at noon, Hellie, so you and me better be in that car by nine," Harry said, as Hellie was taking a tray of dishes to the kitchen.

"I'm already packed, Harry."

"I'll have some breakfast set out at eight and make you some sandwiches for the train," Birdy said.

"Oh, they have a dining car on the train," Harry said, puffing on an after-dinner cigar.

Hellie noticed Birdy's disappointed face and snapped, "It isn't any *trouble*, Harry. It's a courtesy."

"Oh, well, sure. Thanks, Birdy."

Lizzie and Hellie did the dishes, giving Birdy a break. She really wasn't used to kitchen work, which she had been doing in addition to her regular household chores while the search for a new cook was on.

"I don't want you to go," Lizzie said, the steam from the kitchen sink fogging the overhead window. "I thought we had a pact. What'd you say? Be a good double-team?"

"I know," Hellie said, holding her hand under the stream of warm water. "But blood is thicker than this stuff."

"I know," Lizzie said. "Still . . ."

"Look, Lizzie, we'll always be friends, okay? We can write and maybe even use the telephone if you can talk Mrs. G. into it. Harry says we have money now, so you can call me collect."

"Without you, that ol' witch will walk all over me," she said.

"Well, don't you let her. You stand up for your rights just fine now, Lizzie. Look how far you've come since we met back east. I'll bet you haven't even thought about your old doll Mary in months. Bet you don't even know where she is."

"No fun without you, Hellsbells." Then, "Gee, you think maybe you'll go back to New York and find you hate it there now and maybe you'll come back? Think maybe you'll miss silver polish, dirty diapers, ironing boards, and cow shit?"

"You mean bullshit," Hellie said, nudging her.

"Yes, that too," Lizzie said, laughing.

The rest of their talk was light reminiscences from their journey together. They vowed the real good-bye would be in the morning over breakfast, but Hellie had a feeling this was the real good-bye, right here, over damp dish towels and wrapped leftovers from their last dinner together.

Hellie didn't sleep well at all. Her room seemed to be filled with ghosts, yanking her awake, keeping her tossing and turning. She finally gave in, got up, made her bunk, then sat on top and read.

She went through her drawers to make sure she hadn't forgotten anything. There was Slim, hanging off a hook in her closet. Good ol' Slim, she thought. How many times had Slim saved the day? She opened her valise to add the slingshot to her things. There, on top, was Mary, Lizzie's precious doll. Hellie reached in and picked up the poppet, worn, almost faceless from years of love. She smiled and returned it to its place on top of the valise.

She took Slim and placed it on the pillow of her crisply made bunk, knowing Lizzie would find it. Fair enough trade, she thought. Security for security . . . even though all her attempts to teach Lizzie how to shoot were hopeless, even though she herself had never owned a doll and actually teased those girls who did when she was younger. Fair enough trade.

She stacked her things neatly on the porch of the washhouse and walked to the kitchen, where she found her breakfast waiting under a warm napkin but no one there to share it with.

Harry stomped into the kitchen. "Hurry up, Hellie. That old car was hard to start and I left it running. I got your stuff. Down that coffee and let's get gone."

There was a basket with sandwiches, but Lizzie, Birdy, Mrs. G., and Joey were nowhere to be seen or heard.

"Where is everybody?" she asked Harry.

"Oh, something about the old lady upstairs needing some help or something. Birdy said to say good-bye."

"Lizzie?" Hellie asked.

"She's upstairs, too. Come on, Hellie. It's after nine. We miss that train we're stuck in this podunk another three days."

The cold air greeted her with the first flake of snow.

54

"Bet you can't wait to put some distance between you and that sweatshop," Harry said, as he ground the gears until he found reverse. He picked up one of her chafed, red, washerwoman hands. "Look at those." He struggled finding a gear, and Hellie eased it into place.

"Don't tell me you drive now, too," Harry said. "Look out, New York!"

Hellie looked at the washhouse as they passed it, the smokehouse, the icehouse, the barns, the bunkhouse. She remembered her first impression of all this, her thoughts of being rich, only to be dashed by the life assigned her in the washhouse. *Sure, good riddance,* she thought. *Sure.*

Their trip down the long drive toward the county road was silent. *Don't look back, don't look back,* Hellie told herself. But before they rounded the last bend of the drive, she turned and watched the green of the Hidden Hills vanish and slowly turn into the golds and browns of the churned-up earth and used-up pastures, soon to be downy fields of white. She found she didn't have much to say and just counted the five hundred and sixteen electricity poles to Pendleton.

"You stay here with our grip and I'll go get us the tickets," Harry said.

Hellie looked around the station, remembering her first impression of Pendleton from the platform. The fear in Lizzie's face, the excitement in Amanda's voice, the victory in Bergeson's walk, the steel of Mrs. Gorence's eyes.

The oaks and poplars that shaded the town in summer were leafless and defenseless now against the snow. Did the wind really blow the snow into drifts that could cover a barn, like Perry said? Did the rivers and streams really freeze solid, and could you really hear wolves howling from miles away?

"Got you a sleeper and me one, too," Harry said, showing Hellie the tickets.

"What's a sleeper?" Hellie asked.

"We each got a little room all to ourself. No sleeping in the seats. I told you, Hellie, nothing but first class for us from now on. Say, we got some time. I know! Come on, I'll buy you a near beer. I know a good place. Rainbow Cafe."

Hellie knew the place and entered through the side door and sat at the back lunch counter, avoiding the people in the bar area. She knew the small mark she'd made on Pendleton wasn't necessarily a stellar one, and she hoped she wouldn't see the lady from the Rexall or the sheriff.

She ordered a coffee and waited for Harry. He came in through the main entrance, talked to the man behind the bar, then came back with a near beer and a mug.

"Don't you want this?" he asked, looking at her coffee.

"No, coffee is fine."

"Take a sip of this," he said, offering her the mug of gourmet elixir.

She smelled it and said, "No, thanks. That stuff isn't legal, you know."

"As though the law ever stopped Hellie Jondoe." He nudged her and took a seat. "You want anything to eat?"

"I'll have one of Birdy's sandwiches when we're on the train," Hellie said.

"Oh, I gave all that to a porter," Harry said, grabbing a menu off the salt and pepper rack. "I wonder what's good here."

"I don't like it here. There's an old geezer over there just staring at us."

Harry looked toward the bar. "Where?"

"There. In that booth."

Harry looked, and when their eyes met, the old man got up. Hellie knew by his swagger he was more than old and crippled. He was drunk.

He stood in the archway of the cafe. "I thought it was you," he said, looking at Harry.

"Oh yeah, I remember you. What'd the bartender call you? Oregon's oldest juvenile delinquent?"

The man reeked of booze and swayed from side to side. "Yeah, I thought it was you," he said again, this time more challenging.

"Don't you and your pal have some horse tails to tie?" Harry said, dismissing the man and returning to his mug.

"Ace is dead," he growled.

The bartender came over and said, "Come on, Arnie. Come back and sit down. I'll get you a sandwich. Come on. Leave that kid alone."

"No!" he said. "He did it! He brought that flu here! Killed Ace! He did! You forgetting how god-awful sick you got?"

"Come on, Hellie," Harry said, taking her arm and ushering her toward the door. "Let's wait at the station."

The chill of the air felt good on Hellie's face as they walked toward the station.

"I can't wait to get us out of this dump," Harry said.

They turned a corner and walked into Arnie Meeker. This time he had a gun in his hand.

Hellie gasped and Harry took a step back.

"Don't matter to me if they hang me or not," Arnie said.

"Hey, old-timer," Harry said, "watch where you're pointing that thing, huh?"

Arnie's hand shook. The pistol was aimed at Harry's face. Harry was frozen.

Without a thought to the wiser, Hellie stepped between the man and Harry. "Come on, mister. You don't want to hurt anybody," she said. The man glanced from Harry to Hellie. His eyes were red and tear-filled.

"He got Ace sick!" he said, keeping the gun on Harry.

"I know. Lots of us got sick. But, come on. Give me the gun."

"Hellie, let me handle this," Harry said. "He's just the town drunk. Look at him shake."

"You don't move!" Arnie said, tears now rolling down his face.

Hellie put her hands out and encased the gun, now pointed toward her chest. "Please, mister. Give me the gun. Now, you don't want to shoot me, do you? Heck, I'm just a kid." His trembling telegraphed down his arm, charged through the pistol and into Hellie's body.

They locked eyes. Slowly, he released the gun.

"Thank you," Hellie whispered, taking the gun, now feeling her heart thunder down to her toes.

Arnie ran a gnarled hand over his face. "Me and Ace been friends since we was two," he said. "God, I miss him."

And with that, he turned and, hump-shouldered, shuffled back toward the Rainbow Cafe.

Hellie turned and looked at Harry, who was ashen and grasping for air. "You okay?"

"Hellie, didn't I teach you never to step in front of a gun?" he managed, leaning against a tree for support.

They heard the whistle of the train as it approached Pendleton. "Come on, Hellie. We're getting out of this jerkwater town."

"What do I do with this?" she asked, looking at the gun.

Harry took the old gun. "Look at this thing. So rusty I bet it wouldn't even have gone off. Stupid old man." He tossed it into the bushes and said, "Come on. We got a train to catch."

There were only a few people in the car, so they had a set of seats to themselves. Hellie sat opposite Harry.

"That was some little show back there, wasn't it?" Harry said. "You and me, Hellie. What a team. But you know, Hellie, sometimes you disappoint me."

"Why?"

"You can honestly sit there and tell me you never found that ol' lady's wall safe?" He shook his head and added a stately, "Tsk, tsk, tsk." Then, "Reach under your seat and open that satchel."

Hellie found the satchel under her train seat. She opened it and looked down at the money, neatly bundled.

Harry grinned at her. "While you've been learning how to be a washerwoman, I've been practicing." He blew on his fingertips. "It's all in the touch."

Hellie closed the satchel and looked out onto the train platform.

"I can't believe you did this," she finally said.

"I can't believe you *didn't*," he returned.

"But that's out and out stealing," she said.

"Geez, Hellie, when did you grow a conscience?" he asked, trying to jolly the old Hellie back.

Hellie looked at the satchel's silver handle, which was engraved "T.B.G."

Then, out of his coat pocket Harry pulled a pearl-handled pistol. "Here. Got you a little bonus. What the hell good a gun does locked in a safe, I'll never know."

Hellie took it. "Just like the one I shot Archie with," she whispered.

"Yeah. That's why I thought you'd like it. That was some fight, eh, Hellie? But you and me won."

"Yeah. But I killed a kid . . ."

"So what? I took a bullet."

"And I almost took a bullet for you, today. I think that makes us just about even, doesn't it, Harry?"

They stared at each other as the conductor came through the car. "Five minutes," he stated flatly as he walked through. "All ashore who's going ashore."

He looked down and saw the pistol in Hellie's lap and said, "Kindly stow your weapon, Miss."

Hellie didn't respond, but just stared coolly at her brother.

Finally, Harry got up and said, "Look, I got to use the men's room."

When he returned, Hellie, her valise, and the money-filled satchel were gone. Harry saw Hellie on the platform. He ran to the stairwell and shouted down to her. "Get on this train! I didn't come all this way just to go back empty-handed."

"Go home, Harry." She took a step back from a gush of steam.

"Hellie, what I got is yours and what you got . . ."

"Is still *mine!*"

"Those tears I see? Hellie Jondoe is crying?"

"I do it all the time, now," she said back to him.

"Hellie, we're kin."

"So are they," she said, ticking her head east toward the Hidden Hills.

"Don't be stupid, Hellie. Get on this train. I got us all set up."

"I'm not stupid, Harry."

"Train's moving, Hellie." He offered his hand. She stopped walking, smiled, and shook her head no as the train lurched forward.

Yelling now, Harry leaned out and said, "Just for that I'm not going to tell you . . ."

"Tell me what?" she called against the noise of the train.

"*I* killed Archie!"

He flashed his smile and waved as the train pulled out. Hellie watched him step back inside the shadows of the stairwell.

"Good-bye, Harry," she whispered. She slung her valise over one shoulder, the satchel over the other, and dragged the leather case down off the platform.

Arla's old Model T fought her tooth and nail and the snow nearly hid the road, but two hours later she drove up the drive of the Hidden Hills, now resplendent in a quilt of white.

She entered through the front entrance and, toting only the satchel, went straight upstairs and entered Mrs. Gorence's room. "I have something to . . ." She stopped.

"Hellsbells!" Lizzie whispered loudly, her face alight. "You came . . ."

"Sssh!" Birdy admonished.

Mrs. Gorence seemed to have shrunk overnight. Her tiny form barely made an outline in the bed—just two sticks for legs. She was propped up, but even the usually forgiving dim light didn't soften the lines of weary pain on her small face.

"She dying?" Hellie asked Birdy.

Mrs. Gorence opened her eyes and said, "No, I'm not dying! Who asked that?" Her eyes landed on Hellie. "Oh. You."

Birdy said, "She needs to rest, Hellie. Say your good-byes and then just leave, okay?"

"Turn on some lights," Mrs. Gorence barked, as she struggled to sit up higher in her bed. "Lizzie. Tend to Joey. Birdy, fly away."

"You know the doctor said you should rest and save your energy," Birdy said.

"Save my energy for what, breaking horses?"

"Save your energy so you can get over this bout," Birdy said, matching the tone in Mrs. Gorence's voice.

"Just so I can get ready for the next one? No thanks. Wish I'd caught that damn flu!" She looked to the heavens and said, "But that would have been just too easy, eh, Lord?"

"Doctor Cornell said just a few days' rest and . . ."

"Since when do we listen to that quack? And didn't I ask you and Lizzie to leave?" Then, she shouted, "Evaporate!" That left her coughing. "Not you, Hellie."

Hellie pointed to the satchel. "That's . . ."

"I know what that is," she snarled, breaking her off. "You picked the lock on the wall safe. Robbed me blind!"

"Safecracking is one of Harry's skills."

She looked up at Hellie and fingered her lace counterpane. "Oh. Your brother." She looked away and said, "My own fault for trusting him."

"He took it, but I took it back. Your pistol's in there, too."

"And I suppose you want my eternal gratitude. A reward, perhaps, before you catch your train?" She voice was weak, but icy.

"I don't walk out on my contracts," Hellie said.

"Contracts?"

"That indenture thing. Remember?"

"Of course I remember and don't take that tone with me. But as it so happens, your brother bought your indenture. That's why I consented to let you go. So go. You're free."

"So, how much is my indenture?"

"One hundred and fifty dollars. Why?"

"And how much did you write down I still owe you for my police rap?"

"Seventy."

Hellie's face frowned as she ran the figures and used her fingers to count by ten.

"Don't strain yourself," said Mrs. Gorence. "That's two hundred and twenty dollars. Your brother paid me two-fifty. We're all clear. Even-steven. More than even-steven. So you can go with a clean record and a clear conscience."

"Nobody pays my way." Hellie pointed to the satchel. "You can keep that two-fifty for the trouble I caused you, but I'll pay my own bills, thank you very much." She looked out the window, then added, "But it so happens, I'm on reduced circumstances right now. So, I guess I'll just have to stay here and work it off. Like it says in that indenture."

Mrs. Gorence looked up at Hellie, sniffed, and said, "Well, then. Since you're being such a god-awful saint about it, I have no choice but to accept your offer."

"Good, because I still have that hillside to finish clearing. One wringer is broke, so I have to fix that. There's some old frames in the silver room that need polishing. And Birdy says those leg exercises she's done for Joey are working real good, so I thought we'd try a few on you, so's you can junk that cane. It makes you look like a rickety old woman."

"I *am* a rickety old woman," she snapped.

"Well, no use advertising it."

"Are you finished?" Mrs. Gorence asked, the tiniest trace of a smile on her face, the faintest bit of a spark in her eyes.

"Oh, I haven't even started. How can I teach Joey to ride a horse unless I know how, and then I was thinking about Lizzie."

Hellie sat on the edge of the bed, but when she felt Mrs. Gorence's cool glance, she quickly got up and smoothed the cover.

"What about Lizzie?"

"Well, once we get you back on your feet, we need to be thinking about that eye of hers. Then, there's that photograph stuff."

"What photograph stuff?" she asked.

"Oh, didn't I tell you? I'm learning me how to take pictures and write up stories to go with them."

"'Learning me'?" she mocked.

"Well, sure, I'll learn you, too," Hellie answered. "One thing at a time. First you. Getting you on your feet." Their eyes met. "Now," Hellie added, "will you be coming down for your lunch, or will I be bringing you up a tray?"

"I'll be coming down." She leaned over and tried to grasp her leather leg brace, standing at attention next to her bedpost.

"Need help?" Hellie asked, moving the brace just a little farther.

"No, I don't! Look here, you little guttersnipe!" They locked eyes as they had nearly every day of their brief acquaintance. Mrs. Gorence was the first to break with a craggy smile. "All right, Hellie Jondoe. *Kindly* lend me a hand."

Epilogue

July 9, 1919

Dear Harry,

I enclose two photographs. We have a drugstore in town that develops the negatives, but I want to learn how to do that someday myself. And look, I learned typewriting. Mrs. G. got me one for my birthday, which we have decided is May First. I am now officially fourteen, give or take.

The first photo is of folks you remember—Lizzie, Joey, Birdy, Perry, and Mrs. G. It might be odd to have a picnic in a graveyard, but that's what we do, now and then.

The second photo is of me. I set it up and Lizzie pushed the shutter button.

Harry, I'm sorry this letter can't find you under better sircom . . . sircomstan . . . conditions. Please keep these photos as reminders that your sister is fine. And write when you can. But Harry, please do not come west when you are released. You are so smart, but you never got wise. Never learned to plow around the stumps, as we say here in the west. Maybe Sing Sing will change your mind and you'll find some way to a better life. Maybe you should get yourself on an orphan train. Ha ha.

> Your sister,
> Hellie

> P.S. I will send you a copy of my side of the orphan train story when the Hearst man puts it out. Who knows? Maybe someday your sister will be famous!

Glossary

afterpiece   one's rear end

amputate   to depart, to run away from crime

annex   to steal

Astorbilt   a rich person—a combination of the names Astor and Vanderbilt

avenoodles   those who live on 5th Avenue, New York City

the baby-act   a plea of innocence because of youth

beanery   a cheap eating house

below (above) the line   the bad part of New York City, 14th Street

blow-back   to return stolen goods to the victim

boyo   a boy, a lad, a friendly way of referring to a man, chum, pal—primarily Irish

brace (game)   a crooked card game, any con

cannon   a pickpocket, especially a good one

Chinaman's chance   no chance at all

Chinee   a Chinese person

chronic   a drug addict

chump   a mark, a sucker

clam up   to keep quiet

claw   a pickpocket

clock and sling   a watch and chain

coast   to be under the influence of drugs

cock of the walk   the leader, the one in charge—reference comes from cockfighting

convert   a new drug addict

coot   idiot, dummy

cop one's take   to sell stolen goods

cow-hick   a bumpkin, a rural oaf

cruiser   a street thug

customer   the victim of a crime

cut a melon   to divvy up the money

daisyville   the country, the hicks

rabbit (dead rabbit)   a street thug

the dimes   money, cash

dope gun   a syringe used for shooting drugs

double-team   for two to work together in crime

dough bug   a rich person

drop   to kill with a gun

drop   a place to hide, retrieve, or sell stolen goods; the act of doing this

evaporate   to leave, flee, vanish

fag   a cigarette or butt of a cigarette

Fagin   a teacher of crime

fall   to be arrested; an arrest

fence   a person who receives or buys stolen goods

field marshal   the leader of a gang

fin   five dollars

fleece   to steal or cheat

fleet   a gang of thieves, thugs

flimp   to pickpocket

flophouse (flop)   a bed, place to sleep

fruit   an easy mark, a sucker, one who is "ripe" and easy pickings

funker   a lowly thief, a common thug

gang in (with)   to form a gang

get the collar   to be arrested

glassy eye   a drug addict

go down blazing   to die in a shootout

God's medicine   morphine

gopher   a young thief, a small thief who can get into small places

goonlet   a young hood

grift   crime in general, a robbery

grifter   an adventurer-thief

gutterpup, guttersnipe   a young bum or waif

hansom (cab)   a small cab for two passengers with the driver riding on top

holding heavy   having money, in a rich state

hooker   a prostitute

hophead   a dope addict

hype stick   a needle used for drugs

in (on) the plush   living well, high on the hog

in wrong   not included in the gang's inner circle

Jesus-shouter   a preacher

jilt   to leave one's lover

joker   a dose of morphine, the needle and syringe

junkhound   a drug addict

junkie   a drug addict and/or drug pusher

kid's pen   a reform school

king   to lead a gang

lah-de-dah   phony, fancy

lay   the physical place for a planned crime

lead pipe cinch   a sure thing

lift   to steal, to shoplift

Lizzie boy   a gay man

loot   plunder from a crime

lure   one who is used as bait, especially for a crime

lysol dump   a hospital

mark   one's signature

mark   the intended victim of a crime

Mary   morphine

mazuma   money, cash

mission squawker   an evangelist working in the missions

moll   a gangster's girlfriend

moveable property   anything that can be pickpocketed, such as watch,
    hanky, wallet

mug   one's face

needle   a drug addict; injected drugs in general

nursery   a reform school

on the wake   is willing (awake) to illegal activities, open to the idea of crime

panhandle   to ask for money or food, to beg

peeper   a peeping Tom, one who eavesdrops or spies

piece   a gun, weapon

plug ugly   being street tough, named after a New York City street gang in
    the 1800s

prop   a diamond stickpin or other piece of fine jewelry

pudding   an easy job, an easy theft

punk   a worthless man, hoodlum

rake   one's share of the spoils, to share the spoils

sap   a fool, dummy

score   the booty, the stolen goods

score   to commit a crime, to rob, to con

shill   a decoy for a gambler or a hawker

shoot up   to inject drugs

short ear   a rowdy person

sidewalk committee   a gang of pickpockets or thugs

Sing Sing   a large, old prison in Ossining, New York

sinker   a crook who doesn't share his loot with his gang

skin game   a setup game, where one can't win

slice   a portion of the loot, one's share of the goods

slick article   a tricky person

slum   to visit places below one's dignity, to go to the cheap side of town

smacker   one dollar

spot(ted)   to recognize or identify, to be identified

square shooter   an honest person

stab the law   to commit minor crimes

string   a gang; usually with a number preceding, such as "a five string"

suffragettes   women who work for women's right to vote

swell   a well-dressed gentleman

take   the money received by cheating

thimble   a watch

throw in   to join up with

toe the line   to be ready for one's work, to do the job

tote   to carry something, to carry a weapon

tribe   one's gang, a group of thieves or tramps

two-fer   two for the price of one

uncle (for example, Uncle Abe)   a pawnbroker

velvet   profit, easy winnings

wart   a jerk, a creep

weed (out)   to hold back some of the booty, to embezzle small, undetectable amounts

wire   a pickpocket, to pickpocket

I wish to acknowledge two authors. First, Bill Gulick, for showing me the results of perseverance sprinkled with humility and humor. Second, Jane Kirkpatrick, for taking the time, casting a new light, and, like Bill, being a true professional. Thank you, Bill. Thank you, Jane. You're the best!